'It's not every day you get offered a million dollars.' Estelle could at least be honest about that. **'Nor move to Marbella…'**

'You will love it,' Raúl said. 'The night life is fantastic…'

He didn't know her at all, Estelle realised. 'I just hope everyone believes us,' she said.

'Why wouldn't they? Even when we divorce we'll maintain the lie. You understand the confidentiality clause?' Raúl checked. 'No one is ever to know that this is a marriage of convenience only.'

'No one will ever hear it from me,' she assured him. The prospect of being found out was abhorrent to Estelle. 'Just a whirlwind romance and a marriage that didn't work out.'

'Good,' he said. 'And, Estelle, even if we do get on—even if you do like—'

'Don't worry, Raúl,' she interrupted. 'I'm not going to be falling in love with you.' She gave him a tight smile. 'I'll be out of your life as per the contract.'

Carol Marinelli recently filled in a form where she was asked for her job title and was thrilled, after all these years, to be able to put down her answer as 'writer'. Then it asked what Carol did for relaxation and, after chewing her pen for a moment, Carol put down the truth—'writing'. The third question asked, 'What are your hobbies?' Well, not wanting to look obsessed or, worse still, boring, she crossed the fingers on her free hand and answered 'swimming and tennis'. But, given that the chlorine in the pool does terrible things to her highlights, and the closest she's got to a tennis racket in the last couple of years is watching the Australian Open, I'm sure you can guess the real answer!

Recent titles by the same author:

PLAYING THE DUTIFUL WIFE
BEHOLDEN TO THE THRONE*
BANISHED TO THE HAREM*
AN INDECENT PROPOSITION

linked titles

THE PLAYBOY OF PUERTO BANÚS

BY
CAROL MARINELLI

First published in Great Britain 2013
by Mills & Boon, an imprint of Harlequin (UK) Limited.
Harlequin (UK) Limited, Eton House, 18-24 Paradise Road,
Richmond, Surrey TW9 1SR

© Carol Marinelli 2013

ISBN: 978 0 263 90050 7

Harlequin (UK) policy is to use papers that are natural, renewable and recyclable products and made from wood grown in sustainable forests. The logging and manufacturing process conform to the legal environmental regulations of the country of origin.

Printed and bound in Spain
by Blackprint CPI, Barcelona

THE PLAYBOY OF
PUERTO BANÚS

For Anne and Tony
Thank you for all your love and support.
It means so much.
C xxxx

CHAPTER ONE

'ESTELLE, I PROMISE, you wouldn't have to do anything except hold Gordon's hand and dance....'

'And?' Estelle pushed, pulling down the corner on the page she was reading and closing her book, hardly able to believe she was having this conversation, let alone considering going along with Ginny's plan.

'Maybe a small kiss on the cheek or lips...' As Estelle shook her head Ginny pushed on. 'You just have to look as if you're madly in love.'

'With a sixty-four-year-old?'

'Yes.' Ginny sighed, but before Estelle could argue further broke in, 'Everyone will think you're a gold-digger, that you're only with Gordon for his money. Which you will be...' Ginny stopped talking then, interrupted by a terrible coughing fit.

They were housemates rather than best friends, two students trying to get through university. At twenty-five, Estelle was a few years older than Ginny, and had long wondered how Ginny managed to run a car and dress so well, but now she had found out. Ginny worked for a very exclusive escort agency and had a long-term client— Gordon Edwards, a politician with a secret. Which was why, Ginny had assured her, nothing would happen or be

expected from Estelle if she took Ginny's place as his date
at a very grand wedding being held this evening.

'I'd have to share a room with him.'

Estelle had never shared a room with a man in her life.
She wasn't especially shy or retiring but she certainly had
none of Ginny's confidence or social ease. Ginny thought
the weekends were designed for parties, clubs and pubs,
whereas Estelle's idea of a perfect weekend was looking
around old churches or ruins and then curling up on the
sofa with a book.

Not playing escort!

'Gordon always takes the sofa when we share a room.'

'No.' Estelle pushed up her glasses and returned to her
book. She tried to carry on reading about the mausoleum
of the first Qin Emperor but it was terribly hard to do so
when she was so worried about her brother and he *still*
hadn't rung to let her know if he had got the job.

There was no mistaking the fact that the money would
help.

It was late Saturday morning in London, and the wedding was being held that evening in a castle in Scotland. If
Estelle was going to go then she would have to start getting
ready now, for they would fly to Edinburgh and then take
a helicopter to the castle and time was fast running out.

'Please,' Ginny said. 'The agency are freaking because
they can't get anyone suitable at such short notice. He's
coming to pick me up in an hour.'

'What will people think?' Estelle asked. 'If people are
used to seeing him with you…'

'Gordon will take care of that. He'll say that we had an
argument, that I was pushing for an engagement ring or
something. We were going to be finishing soon anyway,
now that I'm nearly through university. Honestly, Estelle,
Gordon really is the loveliest man. There's so much pres-

sure on him to appear straight—he simply cannot go to this wedding without a date. Just think of the money!'

Estelle couldn't stop thinking about the money.

Attending this wedding would mean that she could pay her brother's mortgage for an entire month, as well as a couple of his bills.

Okay, it wouldn't entirely solve their dilemma, but it would buy Andrew and his young family a little bit more time and, given all they had been through this past year, and all that was still to come, they could certainly use the reprieve.

Andrew had done so much for her—had put his own life on hold to make sure that Estelle's life carried on as normally as possible when their parents had died when Estelle was seventeen.

It was time for Estelle to step up, just as Andrew had.

'Okay.' Estelle took a deep breath and her decision was made. 'Ring and say that I'll come.'

'I've already told him that you've agreed,' Ginny admitted. 'Estelle, don't look at me like that. I know how badly you need the money and I simply couldn't bear to tell Gordon that I didn't have someone else lined up.'

Ginny looked more closely at Estelle. Her long black hair was pulled back in a ponytail, her very pale skin was without a blemish, and there was no last night's make-up smudged under Estelle's green eyes because Estelle rarely wore any. Ginny was trying not to show it but she was actually more than a little nervous as to what a made-up Estelle would look like and whether or not she could carry it off.

'You need to get ready. I'll help with your hair and things.'

'You're not coming near me with that cough,' Estelle said. 'I can manage.' She looked at Ginny's doubtful expression. 'We can all look like tarts if we have to.' She smiled and Ginny laughed. 'Though I don't actually have anything I can wear…would anyone notice if I wore something of yours?'

'I bought a new dress for the wedding.' Ginny headed to the wardrobe in her bedroom and Estelle followed.

Estelle's jaw dropped when she held the flimsy gold fabric up.

'Does that go under the dress?'

'It looks stunning on.'

'On *you*, perhaps…' Estelle said, because Ginny was a lot slimmer and had a tiny pert bust, whereas, though small, Estelle was curvy. 'I'm going to look like…'

'Which is the whole point.' Ginny grinned. 'Honestly, Estelle, if you just relax you'll have fun.'

'I doubt it,' Estelle said, wrapping her long dark hair in heated rollers at Ginny's dressing table, and setting to work on her face under her housemate's very watchful eye. Gordon was supposed to be a womanizer, and somehow Estelle had to get the balance right between looking as if she adored him while being far, far too young for him too.

'You need more foundation.'

'More?' Estelle already felt as if she had an inch on.

'And lashings of mascara.'

Ginny watched as Estelle took out the heated rollers and her long dark hair tumbled into ringlets. 'Okay, loads of hairspray…' Ginny said. 'Oh, and by the way, Gordon calls me Virginia, just in case anyone mentions me.'

Ginny blinked a few times when Estelle turned around. The smoky grey eyeshadow and layers of mascara brought out the emerald in her green eyes, and the make-up accentuated Estelle's full lips. Seeing the long black curls framing her friend's petite face, Ginny started to believe that Estelle could carry this off.

'You look amazing! Let's see you in the dress.'

'Won't I change there?'

'Gordon's schedule is too busy. Once you land I would imagine you'll be straight into the wedding.'

The dress was beautiful—sheer and gold, it clung everywhere. It was far too revealing but it was delicious too. Ginny gaped when Estelle wobbled on very high shoes.

'I think Gordon might dump me.'

'This,' Estelle said firmly, 'is a one-off.'

'That's what I said when I first started at the agency,' Ginny admitted. 'But if it goes well…'

'Don't even *think* it!' Estelle said as a car tooted in the street.

'You'll be fine,' Ginny said as Estelle nearly jumped out of her skin. 'You look stunning. I know you can do this.'

Estelle clung onto that as she stepped out of her cheap student accommodation home. Teetering on the unfamiliar high heels, she walked out of the drive and towards a sleek silver car, more than a little terrified to meet the politician.

'I have amazing taste!'

Gordon greeted her with a smile as his driver held open the door and Estelle climbed in. He was chubby, dressed in full Scottish regalia, and he made her smile even before she'd properly sat down.

'And you've got far better legs than me! I feel ridiculous in a kilt.'

Instantly he made her relax.

As the car headed for the airport he brought Estelle up to speed. 'We met two weeks ago…'

'Where?' Estelle asked.

'At Dario's…'

'Dario who?'

Gordon laughed. 'You really don't know anything, do you? It's a bar in Soho—sugar daddy heaven.'

'Oh, God…' she groaned.

'Do you work?' Gordon asked.

'Part-time at the library.'

'Maybe don't mention that. Just say you do a little bit of modelling,' Gordon suggested. 'Keep it all very vague, or say that right now keeping Gordon happy is a full-time job.' Estelle blushed and Gordon noticed. 'I know. Awful, isn't it? I seem to have created this terrible persona.'

'I'm worried that I shan't be able to pull it off.'

'You'll be fine,' Gordon said, and he went through everything with her again.

They practised their story over and over on the short flight to Edinburgh. He even asked after her brother and niece, and she was surprised that he knew about their plight.

'Virginia and I have become good friends this past year,' Gordon said. 'She was ever so upset for you when your brother had his accident and when the baby was born so unwell…' He gave her hand a squeeze. 'How is she now?'

'Waiting for surgery.'

'Just remember that you're helping them,' Gordon said as they transferred to the helicopter that would take them to the castle where the very exclusive wedding was being held.

As they walked across the immaculate lawn Gordon took her hand and she was grateful to hold onto it. He really was nice—if they had met under any other circumstances she would be looking forward to this evening.

'I can't wait to get inside the castle,' Estelle admitted. She'd already told Gordon she was studying ancient architecture.

'There won't be much time for exploring,' Gordon said. 'We'll be shown to our room and there will just be time

to freshen up and touch up your hair and make-up before
we head down for the wedding.'

'Okay.'

'And just remember,' Gordon said, 'this time tomorrow it will all be over and you'll never have to see any of
them again.'

CHAPTER TWO

THE SOUND OF seagulls and the distant throb of music didn't wake Raúl from his slumber; instead they were the sounds that soothed him when he was startled in his sleep. He lay there, heart pounding for a moment, telling himself it was just a dream, while knowing that it was a memory that had jolted him awake.

The gentle motion of his berthed yacht almost tempted him back to sleep, but then he remembered that he was supposed to be meeting with his father.

Raúl forced his eyes open and stared at the tousled blonde hair on his pillow.

'Buenos días,' she purred.

'Buenos días.' Raúl responded, but instead of moving towards her he turned onto his back.

'What time do we leave for the wedding?'

Raúl closed his eyes at her presumption. He had never actually asked Kelly to join him as his guest, but that was the trouble with dating your PA—she knew your diary. The wedding was to be held this evening in the Scottish Highlands. It was nothing for Raúl to fly from Spain to Scotland for a wedding, but Kelly clearly thought that a few weeks out of his office and in his bed meant she was automatically invited.

'I'll speak to you about that later,' Raúl said, glancing at the clock. 'Right now I have to meet with my father.'

'Raúl…' Kelly turned to him in a move that was suggestive.

'Later,' he said, and climbed out of bed. 'I am supposed to be meeting with him in ten minutes.'

'That wouldn't have stopped you before.'

He took the stairs and walked up onto the deck, picking his way through the debris and the evidence of another wild Raúl Sanchez Fuente party. A maid was already starting the mammoth clean up and she gave a cheery wave to Raúl.

'Gracias,' she said as he gave her a substantial cash bonus without apologising for the mess. She did not mind his excesses—Raúl paid and treated her well, unlike the owners of some of the yachts, who expected her to work without complaint for very little.

Raúl put on his shades and walked along the Puerto Banús marina, where his yacht was moored. Here, Raúl belonged. Here, despite his decadent ways, he fitted in— because he was not the wildest. Raúl could hear a party continuing on, the music throbbing, the sound of laughter and merriment carrying across the sparkling water, and it reminded Raúl why he loved this place. Rarely was it ever silent. The marina was full of luxurious yachts and had the heady scent of filthy money. Ludicrously expensive cars were casually parked, all the fruits of serious wealth were on display here, and Raúl—dishevelled, unshaven and terribly beautiful—blended in well.

A couple of tourists stumbling home from a club nudged each other as Raúl walked past, trying to place him. For he was as good-looking as any film star and clearly he was *someone*. People-watching was a regular activity in Puerto

Banús, for amongst the tourists and locals were the rich, the famous and the notorious too.

Raúl scored two out of three—though he *was* famous in the business world.

Enrique, his driver, was waiting for him, and Raúl climbed in and gave a brief greeting, and then sat silently as he was driven the short distance to the Marbella branch of De La Fuente Holdings. He had no doubt as to what his father wanted to discuss, but his mind was going over what Kelly had just said.

'That wouldn't have stopped you before.'

Before what? Raúl asked himself.

Before he lost interest?

Before the chase had ended?

Before she assumed that a Saturday night would be shared?

Raúl was an island.

An island with frequent visitors and world-renowned parties, an island of endless sun and unlimited luxury, but one who preferred guests not to outstay their welcome, only allowed the superficial. Yes, Raúl was an island, and he intended to keep it that way. He certainly didn't want permanent boarders and he chose not to let anyone get too close.

He would never be responsible again for another's heart.

'I shan't be long,' Raúl told Enrique as the car door was lifted and he climbed out.

Raúl was not looking forward to this conversation, but his father had insisted they meet this morning and Raúl just wanted it over and done with.

'Buenos días.' He greeted Angela, his father's PA. 'What are you doing here on a Saturday?' he asked, because Angela usually flew home to her family for the weekend.

'I am trying to track down a certain Spaniard who said he would be here at eight a.m.,' Angela scolded mildly. She was the one woman who could get away with telling Raúl how it was. In her late fifties, she had been employed by the company for as long as Raúl could remember. 'I've been trying to call you—don't you ever have your phone on?'

'The battery is flat.'

'Well, before you speak with your father I need to go through your diary.'

'Later.'

'No, Raúl. I'm flying home later this morning. This needs to be done now. We also need to sort out a new PA for you—preferably one you *don't* fancy!' Angela was less than impressed with Raúl's brief eye-roll. 'Raúl, you need to remember that I'm going on long service leave in a few weeks' time. If I'm going to train somebody up for you, then I need to get on to it now.'

'Choose someone, then,' Raúl said. 'And you're right; perhaps it would be better if it was someone that I did not fancy.'

'Finally!' Angela sighed.

Yes, after having it pointed out to him on numerous occasions, Raúl was finally accepting that mixing business with pleasure had consequences, and sleeping with his PA was perhaps not such a good idea.

What was it with women? Raúl wondered. Why, once they'd made it to his bed, did they decide that they could no longer both work *and* sleep with him? Raúl could set his watch by it. After a few weeks they would decide, just as Kelly now had, that frequent dates and sex weren't enough. They wanted exclusivity, wanted inclusion, wanted commitment—which Raúl simply refused to give. Kelly would be found another position—or paid off handsomely, if that was what she preferred.

'All your flights and transfers are arranged for this afternoon,' Angela said. 'I can't believe that you'll be wearing a kilt.'

'I look good in a kilt.' Raúl smiled. 'Donald has asked that all the male guests wear them. I'm an honorary Scotsman, you know!' He was. He had studied in Scotland for four years, perhaps the best four years of his life, and the friendships he had made there had long continued.

Bar one.

His face hardened as he thought of his ex, who would be there tonight. Perhaps he *should* take Kelly after all, or arrive alone and get off with one of his old flames just to annoy the hell out of Araminta.

'Right, let's get this done…'

He went to walk towards his father's office but Angela called him back. 'It might be an idea to have a coffee before you see him.'

'No need,' Raúl said. 'I will get this over with and then go to Sol's for breakfast.' He loved Saturday mornings at Sol's—a beautiful waterfront café that moved you out quickly if you weren't one of the most beautiful. For people like Raúl they didn't even bother with a bill. They wanted his patronage, wanted the energy he brought to the place. Yes, Raúl decided, he would head there next—except Angela was calling him back again.

'Go and freshen up and I will bring you in coffee and a clean shirt.'

Yes, Angela was the only woman who could get away with speaking to him like that.

Raúl went into his own huge office—which was more like a luxurious hotel suite. As well as the office there was a sumptuous bedroom, and both rooms were put to good use. Heading towards the bathroom, he glanced at the bed and was briefly tempted to lie down. He had had two, possibly three hours' sleep last night. But he forced himself on to the bathroom, grimacing when he saw himself in the mirror. He could see now why Angela had been so insistent that he freshened up before facing his father.

Raúl's black eyes were bloodshot. He had forgotten to shave yesterday, so now two days' worth of black growth lined his strong jaw. His usually immaculate jet-black hair was tousled and fell over his forehead, and the lipstick on his collar, Raúl was sure, *wasn't* the colour that Kelly had been wearing last night.

Yes, he looked every inch the debauched playboy that his father accused him of being.

Raúl took off his jacket and shirt and splashed water on his face, and then set about changing, calling out his thanks to Angela when he heard her tell him that she had put a coffee on his desk.

'*Gracias!*' he called, and walked out mid-shave. Angela was possibly the only woman who did not blush at the sight of him without a shirt—she had seen him in nappies, after all. 'And thanks for pointing me in this direction before I meet with my father.'

'No problem.' She smiled. 'There is a fresh shirt hanging on the chair in your office also.'

'Do you know what it is that he wants to see me about?' Raúl was fishing. He knew exactly what his father would want to discuss. 'Am I to be given another lecture about taming my ways and settling down?'

'I'm not sure.' Only now did Angela's cheeks turn pink. 'Raúl, please listen to what your father has to say, though. This is no time for arguments. Your father is sick…'

'Just because he is ill, it does not necessarily make him right.'

'No,' Angela said carefully. 'But he does care for you, Raúl, even if he does not easily show it. Please listen to him... He is worried about you facing things on your own...' Angela saw Raúl's frown and stopped.

'I think you *do* know what this is about.'

'Raúl, I just ask that you listen—I can't bear to hear you two fighting.'

'Stop worrying,' Raúl said kindly. He liked Angela; she was the closest thing to a mum he had. 'I have no intention of fighting. I just think that at thirty years of age I don't have to be told my bedtime, and certainly not who I'm going to bed *with...*'

Raúl got back to shaving. He had no intention of being dictated to, but his hand did pause. Would it be such a big deal to let his father think that maybe he was actually serious about someone? Would it hurt just to hint that maybe he was close to settling down? His father was dying, after all.

'Wish me luck.' Raúl's voice was wry as, clean-shaven and bit clearer in the head, he walked past Angela to face his father. He glanced over, saw the tension and strain on her features. 'It will be fine,' he reassured her. 'Look...' He knew Angela would never keep news from his father. 'I *am* seeing someone, but I don't want him getting carried away.'

'Who?' Angela's eyes were wide.

'Just an old flame. We ran into each other again. She lives in England but I'm seeing her at the wedding tonight...'

'Araminta!'

'Stop there...' Raúl smiled. That was all that was needed. He knew the seed had been sewn.

Raúl knocked on his father's door and stepped in.

There should have been flames, he thought afterwards.

Or the smell of sulphur. Actually, there should have been the smell of car fuel and the sound of thunder followed by silence. There should at least have been some warning, as he was walked through the door, that he was returning to hell.

CHAPTER THREE

ESTELLE FELT AS if everyone knew what a fraud she was.

She closed her heavily made-up eyes and dragged in a deep breath. They were standing in the castle grounds, waiting to be led to their seating, and some pre-wedding drinks and nibbles were being served.

Why they hell had she agreed to this?

You know why, Estelle told herself, her resolve hardening.

'Are you okay, darling?' Gordon asked. 'The wedding should start soon.'

He'd been nothing but kind, just as Ginny had promised he would be.

'I'm fine,' Estelle said, and held a little more tightly onto his arm, just as Gordon had told her to do.

'This is Estelle.'

Gordon introduced her to a couple and Estelle watched the slight rise of the woman's eyebrow.

'Estelle, this is Veronica and James.'

'Estelle.' Veronica gave a curt nod and soon moved James away.

'You're doing wonderfully,' Gordon said, squeezing her hand and drawing her away from the mingling wedding guests so that they could speak without being overheard. 'Maybe you just need to smile a bit more,' he suggested gently, 'and, I know it calls for brilliant acting, could you try and look just a little more besotted with me? I've got my terrible reputation with women to think of.'

'Of course,' Estelle said through chattering teeth.

'The gay man and the virgin,' Gordon whispered in her ear. 'If only they knew!'

Estelle's eyes widened in horror and Gordon quickly apologised. 'I was just trying to make you smile,' he said.

'I can't believe that she *told* you!'

Estelle was horrified that Ginny would share something as personal and as sensitive as that. Then again, she could believe it—Ginny found it endlessly amusing that Estelle had never slept with anyone. It wasn't by deliberate choice; it wasn't something she'd actively decided. More that she'd been so shell shocked by her parents' death that homework and books had been her escape. By the time she'd emerged from her grief Estelle had felt two steps behind her peers. Clubs and parties had seemed frivolous. It was ancient ruins and buildings that fascinated her, and when she did meet someone there was always a panic that her virgin status must mean she was looking for a husband. More and more it had become an issue.

Now it would seem it was a joke!

She'd be having strong words with Ginny.

'Virginia didn't say it in a malicious way.' Gordon seemed devastated to have upset her. 'We were just talking one night. I really should never have brought it up.'

'It's okay,' Estelle conceded. 'I guess I am a bit of a rarity.'

'We all have our secrets,' Gordon said. 'And for tonight we both have to cover them up.' He smiled at her strained expression. 'Estelle, I know how hard it was for you to agree to this, but I promise you have nothing to feel nervous about. I'm soon to be a happily married man.'

'I know,' Estelle said. Gordon had told her on the plane about his long-term boyfriend, Frank, and the plans they had made. 'I just can't stand the disapproving looks and that everyone thinks of me as a gold-digger,' she admitted. 'Even though that's the whole point of the night.'

'Stop caring what everyone thinks,' Gordon said.

It was the same as she said to Andrew, who was acutely embarrassed to be in a wheelchair. 'You're right.'

Gordon lifted her chin and she smiled into his eyes. 'That's better.' Gordon smiled back. 'We'll get through this together.'

So Estelle held onto his arm and did her best to look suitably besotted, ignoring the occasional disapproving stare from the other guests, and she was just starting to relax and get into things when *he* arrived.

Till that moment Estelle had thought it would be the bride who would make an entrance, and it wasn't the sight of a helicopter landing that had heads turning—helicopters had been landing regularly since Estelle had got there—no, it was the man who stepped out who held everyone's attention.

'Oh, my, the evening just got interesting,' Gordon said as the most stunning man ducked under the blades and then walked towards the gathering.

He was tall, his thick black hair brushed back and gleaming, and his mouth was sulky and unsmiling. His Mediterranean colouring should surely mean that he'd look out of place wearing a kilt, but instead he looked as if he'd been born to wear one. Lean-hipped and long-limbed, but muscular too, he could absolutely carry it off.

He could carry me off right now, Estelle thought wildly—and wild thoughts were rare for Estelle.

She watched as he accepted whisky from a waiter and then stood still. He seemed removed and remote from everyone else. Even the women who flocked to him were quickly dismissed, as if at any minute he might simply walk off.

Then he met her eyes.

Estelle tried to flick hers away, except she found that she couldn't.

His eyes drifted down over the gold dress, but not in the disapproving way that Veronica's had. Although they weren't approving either. They were merely assessing.

She felt herself burn as his eyes moved then to her sixty-four-year-old date, and she wanted to correct him—wanted to tell him that the rotund, red-faced man who was struggling with the heat in his heavy kilt and jacket was not her lover. Though of course she could not.

She wanted to, though.

'Eyes only for me, darling,' Gordon reminded her, perhaps picking up on the crackle of energy crossing the lawn. His glance followed Estelle's gaze. 'Though frankly no one would blame you a bit for looking. He's completely divine.'

'Who?' Estelle tried to pretend that she hadn't noticed the delicious stranger—Gordon was paying her good money to be here, after all—but she wasn't fooling anyone.

'Raúl Sanchez Fuente,' Gordon said in a low voice. 'Our paths cross now and then at various functions. He owns everything but morals. The bastard even looks good in a kilt. He has my heart—not that he wants it…'

Estelle couldn't help but laugh.

Raúl's eyes lazily worked over the guests. He was questioning now his decision to come alone. He needed distraction tonight, but when he had thought of the old flames that he might run into he had been thinking of the perky breasts and the narrow waists of yesteryear, as if the clock might

have stopped on his university days. Instead the hands of
time had moved on.

There was Shona. Her once long red hair was now cut
too severely and she stood next to a chinless wonder. She
caught his eye and then blushed unbecomingly and shot
him a furious look, as if their once torrid times could be
erased and forgotten by her wedding ring.

He knew, though, that she was remembering.

'Raúl…'

He frowned when he saw Araminta walking towards
him. She was wearing that slightly needy smile that Raúl
recognised only too well and it made his early warning
system react—because temporary distraction was his re-
quirement tonight, not desperation.

'How are you?'

'Not bad,' she said, and then proceeded to tell him about
her hellish divorce, how she was now single, how she'd
thought about him often since the break-up, how she'd been
looking forward to seeing him tonight, how she regretted
the way things had worked out for them…

'I told you that you would at the time.' Raúl did not do
sentiment. 'You'll have to excuse me. I have to make a call.'

'We'll catch up later, though?'

He could hear the hope in her voice and it irked him.

Was he good enough for her father now? Rich enough?
Established enough?

'There's nothing to catch up on.'

Just like that he dismissed her, his black eyes not even
watching her as she gave a small sob and walked off.

What on earth was he doing here? Raúl wondered. He
should be getting ready to party on his yacht, or to hit the
clubs—should be losing himself instead of getting reac-
quainted with his past. More to the point, there was hardly
a limitless choice of women in this castle in the Scottish

Highlands. And after what Raúl had found out this morning his own company wasn't one he wanted to keep.

His hand tightened on the whisky glass he held. The full impact of what his father had told him was only now starting to hit him.

So black were his thoughts, so sideswiped was he by the revelations, Raúl actually considered leaving—just summoning his pilot and walking out. But then a tumble of dark hair and incredibly pale skin caught his eye and held it. She looked nervous and awkward—which was unusual for Gordon's tarts. They were normally brash and confident. But not this one.

He held her gaze when she caught his and now there was only one woman he wanted to walk towards him—except she was holding tightly to Gordon's arm.

She offered far more than distraction—she offered oblivion. Because for the first time since his conversation with his father he forgot about it.

Perhaps he would stay. At least for the service…

A deep Scottish voice filled the air and the guests were informed that the wedding would soon commence and they were to make their way to their seats.

'Come on.' Gordon took Estelle's hand. 'I love a good wedding.'

'And me.' Estelle smiled.

They walked through the mild night. The grounds were lit by torches and there were chairs set out. With the castle as a backdrop the scene looked completely stunning, and Estelle let go of her guilt, determined to enjoy herself. She'd been on a plane and, for the first time in her life, a helicopter, she was staying the night in a beautiful castle in the Scottish Highlands, and Gordon was an absolute delight. Despite having dreaded it, she was enjoying herself, Estelle realised as they took their seats and she made more small talk with Gordon.

'Donald says that Victoria's so nervous,' he told her. 'She's such a perfectionist, apparently, and she's been stressing over the details for months.'

'Well, it all seems to have paid off,' Estelle said. 'I can't wait to see what she's wearing.'

Just as she'd finally started to relax as the music changed and they all stood for the bride, just as she'd decided simply to enjoy herself, she turned to get a first glimpse of the bride—only to realise that Raúl was sitting behind her.

Directly behind her.

It should make no difference, Estelle told herself. It was a simple coincidence. But even coincidence was too big a word—after all, he had to sit *somewhere*. Estelle was just acutely aware that he was there.

She tried to concentrate on the bride as she made her way to Donald. Victoria really did look stunning. She was wearing a very simple white dress and carried a small posy of heather. The smile on Donald's face as his bride walked towards him had Estelle smiling too—but not for long. She could feel Raúl's eyes burning into her shoulder, and a little while later her scalp felt as if it were on fire. She was sure his eyes lingered there.

She did her best to focus on the service. It was incredibly romantic. So much so that when they got to the 'in sickness and in health' part it actually brought tears to her eyes as she remembered her brother Andrew's wedding, just over a year ago.

Who could have known then the hard blows fate had in store for him and his pregnant bride, Amanda?

Ever the gentleman, Gordon pressed a tissue into her hand.

'Thank you.' Estelle gave a watery smile and Gordon gave her hand a squeeze.

* * *

Please! Raúl thought. *Spare me the crocodile tears.* It had been the same with Gordon's previous girlfriend—what was her name? Raúl smiled to himself, as he had the day they were introduced.

Virginia.

This one, though, even if she wasn't to Raúl's usual taste, was stunning. Raven-haired women were far from a rarity where Raúl came from, and for that reason he certainly preferred a blonde—for variety, two blondes!

He wanted raven tonight.

Turn around, Raúl thought, for he wanted to meet those eyes again.

Turn around, he willed her, watching her shoulders stiffen, watching the slight tilt of her neck as if she was aware of but resisting his silent demand.

How she was resisting.

Estelle sat rigid and then stood in the same way after the service was over, when the bride and groom were letting doves fly. They fluttered high into the sky and the crowd murmured and pointed and turned to watch them in flight.

Reluctantly she also turned, and she must look up, Estelle thought helplessly as two black liquid pools invited her to dive in. She should, like everyone else, move her gaze upwards and watch the doves fly off into the distance.

Instead she faced him.

What the hell are you doing with him? Raúl wanted to ask. *What the hell are you doing with a man perhaps three times your age?*

Of course he knew the answer.

Money.

And Raúl knew then what to do—knew the answer to the dilemma that had been force-fed to him at breakfast-time.

His mouth moved into a smile and he watched as her head jerked away—watched as she stared, too late, up into the sky. And he saw her pale throat as her neck arched and he wanted his mouth there.

A piper led them back to the castle. He walked in front of her and Gordon. Estelle's heels kept sinking into the grass, but it was nothing compared to the feeling of drowning in quicksand when she had been caught in Raúl's gaze.

His kilt was greys and lilacs, his jacket a dark purple velvet, his posture and his stride exact and sensual. She wanted to run up to him, to tap him on the shoulder and tell him to please leave her alone. Yet he had done nothing. He wasn't even looking over his shoulder. He was just chatting with a fellow guest as they made their way back to the castle.

Very deliberately Raúl ignored her. He turned his back and chatted with Donald, asked a favour from a friend, and then flirted a little with a couple of old flames—but at all times he knew that her eyes more than occasionally searched out his.

Raúl knew exactly what he was doing and he knew exactly why.

Mixing business with pleasure had caused a few problems for Raúl in the past.

Tonight it was suddenly the solution.

CHAPTER FOUR

'EXCUSE ME, SIR.'

A waiter halted Estelle and Gordon as they made their way into the Grand Hall and to their table.

'There's been a change to the seating plan. Donald and Victoria didn't realise that you were seated so far back. It's all been rectified now. Please accept our apologies for the mistake.'

'*Oooh,* we're getting an upgrade,' Gordon said as they were led nearer to the front.

Estelle flushed when she saw that the rather teary woman she had seen earlier speaking with Raúl was being quietly shuffled back to the bowels of the hall. Estelle knew even before they arrived at the new table which one it would be.

Raúl did not look up as they made their way over. Not until they were being shown into their seats.

She smiled a greeting to Veronica and James, but could not even attempt one for Raúl—both seats either side of him were empty.

He had done this.

Estelle tried to tell herself she was imagining things, or overreacting, but somehow she knew she was right. Knew that those long, lingering stares had led to this.

The chair next to him was being held out. She wanted

to turn to Gordon, to ask if they could swap seats but she knew that would look ridiculous.

It was a simple change of seating, Estelle told herself.

She acknowledged to herself that she lied.

'Gordon.' Raúl shook his hand.

'Raúl.'

Gordon smiled as he took the seat next to Estelle, so she was sandwiched between them, and she leant back a little as they chatted.

'I haven't seen you since…' Gordon laughed. 'Since last wedding season. This is Estelle.'

'Estelle.' He raised one eyebrow as she took her seat beside him. 'In Spain you would be Estela.'

'We're in England.' She was aware of her brittle response, but her defences were up—though she did try to soften it with a brief smile.

'Of course.' Raúl shrugged. 'Though I must speak with my pilot. He was most insistent, when we landed, that this was *Scotland*.'

She tried so hard not to, but Estelle twitched her lips into a slight smile.

'This is Shona and Henry…' Raúl introduced them as a waiter poured some wine.

Estelle took a sip and then asked for water—for a draughty castle, it felt terribly warm.

There was brief conversation and more introductions taking place, and all would have been fine if Raúl were not there. But Estelle was aware, despite his nonchalant appearance, that he was carefully listening to her responses.

She laughed just a little too loudly at one of Gordon's jokes.

As she'd been told to do.

Gordon was busy speaking with James, and for something to do Estelle looked through the menu, squinting because Ginny had suggested that she leave her glasses at home.

Raúl misconstrued it as a frown.

'Vichyssoise,' came his low, deep voice. 'It is a soup. It's delicious.'

'I don't need hand-holding for the menu.' Estelle stopped herself, aware she was coming across as terribly rude, but her nerves were prickling in defensiveness. 'And you failed to mention it's served cold.'

'No.' He smiled. 'I was just about to tell you that.'

Soup was a terribly hard ask with Raúl sitting next to her, but she worked her way through it, even though her conversation with Gordon kept getting interrupted by his phone.

'I can't even get a night off.' He sighed.

'Important?' Estelle checked.

'It could be soon. I'll have to keep it on silent.'

The main course was served and it was the most gorgeous beef Estelle had ever tasted. Yet it stuck in her throat—especially when Veronica asked her a question.

'Do you work, Estelle?'

She took a drink of water before answering. 'I do a bit of modeling.' Estelle gave a small smile, remembering how Gordon had told her to respond to such a question. She just hadn't expected to be inhaling testosterone when she answered. 'Though, of course, taking care of Gordon is a full-time job...'

Estelle saw the pausing of Raúl's fork and then heard Gordon's stab of laughter. She was locked in a lie and there was no way out. It was an act, Estelle told herself. Just one night and she would never have to see these people again—and what did she care if Raúl thought her cheap?

'Could you pass me the pepper?' came the silk of his voice.

Was it the fact that it had been asked with a Spanish accent that made the question sound sexy, or was it that she was going mad?

She passed it, holding the heavy silver pot and releasing it to him, feeling the brief warmth of his fingertips as he took it. He immediately noticed her error. 'That's the salt,' Raúl said, and she had to go through it again.

It was bizarre. He had said hardly two words to her, had made no suggestions. There were no knees pressing into hers under the table and his hands had not lingered when she'd passed him the pepper, yet the air between them was thick with tension.

He declined dessert and spread cheese onto Scottish oatcakes. 'I'd forgotten how good these taste.'

She turned and watched as he took a bite and then ran his tongue over his lip, capturing a small sliver of quince paste.

'Now I remember.'

There was no implication. He was only making small talk.

It was Estelle's mind that searched every word.

She spread cheese on an oatcake herself and added quince.

'Fantastic?' Raúl asked.

'Yes.'

She knew he meant sex.

'Now the speeches.' Gordon sighed.

They were long. Terribly long. Especially when you had no idea who the couple were. Especially when you were supposed to be paying attention to the man on your right but your mind was on the one to your left.

First it was Victoria's father, who rambled on just a touch too long. Then it was the groom Donald's turn, and he was thankfully a bit quicker—and funnier too. He moved through the formalities and, on behalf of himself and his new wife, especially thanked all who had travelled from afar.

'I was hoping Raúl wouldn't make it, of course,' Donald said, looking over to Raúl, as did the whole room. 'I'm just thankful Victoria didn't see him in a kilt until *after* my ring was on her finger. Trust a Spaniard to wear a kilt so well.'

The whole room laughed. Raúl's shoulders moved in a light, good-natured laugh too. He wasn't remotely embarrassed—no doubt more than used to the attention and to having his beauty confirmed.

Then it was the best man's turn.

'In Spain there are no speeches at a wedding,' Raúl said, leaning across her a little to speak to Gordon.

She could smell his expensive cologne, and his arm was leaning slightly on her. Estelle watched her fingers around the stem of her glass tighten.

'We just have the wedding, a party, and then bed,' Raúl said.

It was the first hint of suggestion, but even so she could merely be reading into things too much. Except as he leant over her to hear Gordon's response Estelle wanted to put her hand up, wanted to ask for the lights to come on, for this assault on her senses to stop, to tell the room the inappropriateness of the man sitting beside her. Only not a single thing had he done—not a word or hand had he put wrong.

So why was her left breast aching, so close to where his arm was? Why were her two front teeth biting down on her lip at the sight of his cheek, inches away?

'Really?' Gordon checked. 'I might just have to move to Spain! In actual fact I was—'

Gordon was interrupted by the buzz of his phone and

Raúl moved back in his seat. Estelle sat watching the newly wed couple dancing.

'Darling, I am so sorry,' Gordon said as he read a message on his phone. 'I am going to have to find somewhere I can make some calls and use a computer.'

'Good luck getting internet access,' drawled Raúl. 'I have to go outside just to make a call.'

'I might be some time.'

'Trouble?' Estelle asked

'Always.' Gordon rolled his eyes. 'Though this is unexpected. But I'll deal with it as quickly as I can. I hate to leave you on your own.'

'She won't be on her own,' Raúl said. 'I can keep an eye.'

She rather wished that he wouldn't.

'Thanks so much,' Gordon said. 'In that dress she deserves to dance.' He turned to Estelle. 'I really am sorry to leave you...' For appearances' sake, he kissed her on the cheek.

What a waste of her mouth, Raúl thought.

Once Gordon had gone she turned to James and Veronica, on her right, desperately trying to feed into their conversation. But they were certainly not interested in Gordon's new date. Over and over they politely dismissed her, and then followed the other couples at their table and got up to dance—leaving her alone with Raúl.

'From the back you could be Spanish...'

She turned to the sound of his voice.

'But from the front...'

His eyes ran over her creamy complexion and she felt heat sear her face as his eyes bored into hers. And though they did not wander—he was far too suave for that—somehow he undressed her. Somehow she sat there on her seat beside him at the wedding as if they were a couple. And when he looked at her, she felt, for a bizarre second, as if she was completely naked.

He was as potent as that.

CHAPTER FIVE

'IRISH?' HE CHECKED, and Estelle hesitated for a moment before nodding.

She did not want to give any information to this man—did not even want to partake in conversation.

'Yet your accent is English?'

'My parents moved to England before I was born.' She gave a tight swallow and hoped her stilted response would halt the conversation. It did not.

'Where in England are they?'

'They're not,' Estelle answered, terribly reluctant to reveal *anything* of herself.

Raúl did not push. Instead he moved the conversation on.

'So, where did you and Gordon meet?'

'We met at Dario's.' Estelle answered the question as Gordon had told her to, trying to tell herself he was just being polite, but every sense in her body seemed set to high alert. 'It's a bar—'

'In Soho,' Raúl broke in. 'I have heard a lot about Dario's.'

Beneath her make-up her cheeks were scalding.

'Not that I have been,' Raúl said. 'As a male, I would perhaps be too young to get in there.' His lips rose in a slight smile and he watched the colour flood darker in her neck and to her ears. 'Maybe I should give it a try...'

He looked more closely at Estelle. She had eyes that were a very dark green and rounded cheeks—she really was astonishingly attractive. There was something rather sweet about her despite the clothes, despite the make-up, and there was an awkwardness that was as rare as it was refreshing. Raúl was not used to awkwardness in the women he dated.

'So, we both find ourselves alone at a wedding…'

'I'm not alone,' Estelle said. 'Gordon will be back soon.' She did not want to ask, but she found herself doing just that as she glanced to the empty chair beside him. 'How come…?' Her voice faded out. There was no polite way to address it.

'We broke up this morning.'

'I'm sorry.'

'Please don't be.' He thought for a moment before continuing. 'Really to say we broke up is perhaps an exaggeration. To break something would mean you had to have something, and we were only going out for a few weeks.'

'Even so…' Still she attempted to be polite. 'Breakups are hard.'

'I've never found them to be,' Raúl said. 'It's the bit before that I struggle with.'

'When it starts to go wrong?'

'No,' Raúl said. 'When it starts to go right.'

His eyes were looking right into hers, his voice was deep and low, and his words interesting—because despite herself she *did* want to know more about this fascinating man. So much so that she found herself leaning in a little to hear.

'When she starts asking what we are doing next weekend. When you hear her saying "Raúl said…" or "Raúl thinks…"' He paused for a second. 'I don't like to be told what I'm thinking.'

'I'm sure you don't.'

'Do you know what I'm thinking now?'

'I wouldn't presume to.' She could hardly breathe, because she was surely thinking the same.

'Would you like to dance?'

'No, thank you,' Estelle said, because it was far safer to stay seated than to self-combust in his arms. He was sinfully good-looking and, more worryingly, she had a sinking feeling as she realised he was pulling her in deeper with each measured word. 'I'll just wait here for Gordon.'

'Of course,' Raúl said. 'Have you met the bride or groom?'

'No.' Estelle felt as if she were being interviewed. 'You're friends with the groom?'

'I went to university with him.'

'In Spain?'

'No, here in Scotland.'

'Oh!' She wasn't sure why, but that surprised her.

'I was here for four years,' Raúl said. 'Then I moved back to Marbella. I still like to come here. Scotland is a very beautiful country.'

'It is,' Estelle said. 'Well, from the little I've seen.'

'It's your first time?'

She nodded.

'Have you ever been to Spain?'

'Last year,' Estelle said. 'Though only for a few days. Then there was a family emergency and I had to go home.'

'Raúl?'

He barely looked up as a woman came over. It was the same woman who had been moved from the table earlier.

'I thought we could dance.'

'I'm busy.'

'Raúl…'

'Araminta.' Now he turned and looked at her. 'If I wanted to dance with you then I would have asked.'

Estelle blinked, because despite the velvet of his voice his words were brutal.

'That was a bit harsh,' Estelle said as Araminta stumbled off.

'Far better to be harsh than to give mixed messages.'

'Perhaps.'

'So…' Raúl chose his words carefully. 'If taking care of Gordon is a full-time job, what do you do in your time off?'

'My time off?'

'When you're not *working*.'

She didn't frown this time. There was no mistake as to what he meant. Her green eyes flashed as she turned to him. 'I don't appreciate the implication.'

He was surprised by her challenge, liked that she met him head-on—it was rare that anyone did.

'Excuse me,' he said. 'Sometimes my English is not so good…'

When it suited him.

Estelle took a deep breath, her hand still toying with the stem of her glass as she wondered how to play this, deciding she would do her best to be polite.

'What work do you do?' She looked at him. She had absolutely no idea about this man. 'Are you in politics too?'

'Please!'

He watched the slight reluctant smile on her lips.

'I am a director for De La Fuente Holdings, which means I buy, improve or build, and then maybe I sell.' Still he watched her. 'Take this castle; if I owned it I would not have it exclusively as a wedding venue but also as a hotel. It is under-utilised. Mind you, it would need a lot of refurbishment. I have not shared a bathroom since my university days.'

She was far from impressed and tried not to show it. Raúl, of course, could not know that she was studying ancient architecture and that buildings were a passion of hers. The castle renovations she had seen were modest, the rooms cold and the bathrooms sparse—as it should be. The thought of this place being modernised and filled to capacity, no matter how tastefully, left her cold.

Unfortunately *he* didn't.

Not once in her twenty-five years had Estelle even come close to the reaction she was having to Raúl.

If they were anywhere else she would get up and leave.

Or, she conceded, if they were anywhere else she would lean forward and accept his mouth.

'So it's your father's business?' Estelle asked, trying to find a fault in him—trying to tell herself that it was his father's money that had eased his luxurious path to perfection.

'No, it was my mother's family business. My father bought into it when he married.' He saw her tiny frown.

'Sorry, you said De La Fuente, and I thought Fuente was *your* surname...'

For an occasional model who picked up men at Dario's she was rather perceptive, Raúl thought. 'In Spain it is different. You take your father's surname first and then your mother's...'

'I didn't know that.' She tried to fathom it. 'How does it work?'

'My father is Antonio Sanchez. My mother was Gabriella De La Fuente.'

'Was?'

'She passed away in a car accident...'

Normally he could just say it. Every other time he revealed it he just glossed over it, moved swiftly on—tonight, with all he had learnt this morning, suddenly he could not.

Every man except Raúl had struggled in the summer heat with full Scottish regalia. Supremely fit, and used to the sun, Raúl had not even broken a sweat. But now, when the castle was cool, when a draught swirled around the floor, he broke into one—except his face drained of colour.

He tried to right himself, reached for water; he had trained his mind not to linger. Of course he had not quite mastered his mind at night, but even then he had trained himself to wake up before he shouted out.

'Was it recent?' Estelle saw him struggle briefly, knew surely better than anyone how he must feel—for she had lost her parents the same way. She watched as he drained a glass of water and then blinked when he turned and the suave Raúl returned.

'Years ago,' he dismissed. 'When I was a child.' He got back to their discussion, refusing to linger on a deeply buried past. 'My actual name is Raúl Sanchez De La Fuente, but it gets a bit long during introductions.'

He smiled, and so too did Estelle.

'I can imagine.'

'But I don't want to lose my mother's name, and of course my father expects me to keep his.'

'It's nice that the woman's name passes on.'

'It doesn't, though,' Raúl said. 'Well, it does for one generation—it is still weighted to the man.' He saw her frown.

'So, if you had a baby…?'

'That's never going to happen.'

'But if you did?'

'God forbid.' He let out a small sigh. 'I will try to explain.'

He was very patient.

He took the salt and pepper she had so nervously passed to him and, heads together, they sat at the table while he made her a small family tree.

'What is your surname?'

'Connolly.'

'Okay, we have a baby and call her Jane…'

How he made her burn. Not at the baby part, but at the thought of the part to get to that.

'Her name would be Jane Sanchez Connolly.'

'I see.'

'And when Jane marries…' he lifted a hand and grabbed a fork as he plucked a name from the ether '…Harry Potter, her daughter…' he added a spoon '…who shall also be called Jane, would be Jane Sanchez Potter. Connolly would be gone!' He looked at her as she worked it out. 'It is simple. At least the name part is simple. It is the fifty years of marriage that might prove hard.' He glanced over to today's happy couple. 'I can't imagine being tied down to another, and I certainly don't believe in love.'

He always made that clear up-front.

'How can you sit at a wedding and say that?' Estelle challenged. 'Did you not see the smile on Donald's face when he saw his bride?'

'Of course I did,' Raúl said. 'I recognised it well—it was the same smile he gave at the last wedding of his I attended.'

She laughed. There was no choice but to. 'Are you serious?'

'Completely,' Raúl said.

Yet he was smiling, and when he did that she felt as if she should scrabble in her bag for sunglasses, because the force of his smile blinded her to all faults—and she was quite positive a man like Raúl had many.

'You're wrong, Raúl.' She refused to play his cynical game. 'My brother got married last year and he and his wife are deeply in love.'

'A year.' He gave a light shrug. 'It is still the honeymoon phase.'

'They've been through more in this year than most have been through in a lifetime.' And she'd never meant to but she found herself opening up to him. 'Andrew, my brother, was in an accident on their honeymoon—a jet ski...'

'Serious?'

Estelle nodded. 'He's now in a wheelchair.'

'That must take a lot of getting used to.' He thought for a moment. 'Is that the family emergency you had to fly home from your own holiday for?'

Estelle nodded. She didn't tell him it had been a trip around churches. No doubt he assumed she'd been hauled out of a club to hear the news. 'I raced home, and, really, since then things have been tough on them. Amanda was already pregnant when they got married...'

She didn't know why she was telling him. Perhaps it was safer to talk than to dance. Maybe it was easier to talk about her brother and the truth than make up stories about Dario's and seedy clubs in Soho. Or perhaps it was the black liquid eyes that invited conversation, the way he moved his chair a little closer so that he could hear.

'Their daughter was born four months ago. The prospect of being a dad was the main thing that kept Andrew motivated during his rehabilitation. Just when we thought things were turning around...'

Raúl watched her green eyes fill with tears, saw her rapid blink as she tried to stem them.

'She has a heart condition. They're waiting till she's a little bit bigger so they can operate.'

He watched pale hands go to her bag and Estelle took out a photo. He looked at her brother, Andrew, and his wife, and a small frail baby with a slight blue tinge to her skin, and he realised that they hadn't been crocodile tears

he had witnessed during the wedding ceremony. He looked
back to Estelle.

'What's her name?'

'Cecelia.'

Raúl looked at her as she gazed at the photo and he
knew then the reason she was here with Gordon. 'Your
brother?' Raúl asked, just to confirm things in his mind.
'Does he work?'

'No.' Estelle shook her head. 'He was self-employed.
He…' She put away the photo, dragged in a breath, could
not stand to think of all the problems her brother faced.

Exactly at that moment Raúl lightened things.

'My legs are cold.'

Estelle laughed, and as she did she blinked as a photographer's camera flashed in her face.

'Nice natural shot,' the photographer said.

'We're not…' Oh, what did it matter?

'I need to move.' He stood. 'And Gordon asked that I
take care of you.' Raúl held out his hand to her. This dance
was more important than she could ever know. This dance
must ensure that tonight she was thinking only of *him*—
that by the time he approached her with his suggestion it
would not seem so unthinkable. But first he had to set the
tone. First he had to make her aware that he knew the sort
of business she was in. 'Would you like to dance?'

Estelle didn't really have a choice. Walking towards the
dance floor, she had the futile hope that the band would
break into something more frivolous than sensuous, but
all hope was gone as his arms wrapped loosely around her.

'You are nervous?'

'No.'

'I would have thought you would enjoy dancing, given
that you two met at Dario's.'

'I do love to dance.' Estelle forced a bright smile, remembered who she was supposed to be. 'It's just a bit early for me.'

'And me,' Raul said as he took her in his arms. 'About now I would only just be getting ready to go out.'

She couldn't read this man. Not in the least. He held her, he was skilled and graceful, but the eyes that looked down at her were not smiling.

'Relax.'

She tried to—except he'd said it into her ear, causing the sensitive skin there to tingle.

'Can I ask something?'

'Of course,' Estelle said, though she would rather he didn't. She just wanted this duty dance to end.

'What are you doing with Gordon?'

'Excuse me?' She could not believe he would ask that—could not think of anyone else who would be so direct. It was as if all pretence had gone—all tiny implications, all conversation left behind—and the truth was being revealed in his arms.

'There is a huge age difference...'

'That's none of your business.' She felt as if she was being attacked in broad daylight and everyone else was just carrying on, oblivious.

'You are twenty, yes?'

'Twenty-five.'

'He was ten years older than I am now when you were born.'

'They're just numbers.'

'We both work in numbers.'

Estelle went to walk off mid-dance, but his grip merely tightened. 'Of course...' He held her so she could feel the lean outline of his body, inhale the terribly masculine scent of him. 'You want him only for his money.'

'You're incredibly rude.'

'I'm incredibly honest,' Raúl corrected. 'I am not criticizing—there is nothing wrong with that.'

'Vete al infierno!' Estelle said, grateful for a Spanish schoolfriend and lunchtimes being taught by her how to curse. She watched his mouth curve as she told him in his own language to go to hell. 'Excuse me,' Estelle said. 'Sometimes my Spanish is not so good. What I mean to say is…'

He pressed a finger to her lips before she could tell him, in her own language and rather more crudely, exactly where he could go.

The contact with her mouth, the sensual pressure, the intimacy of the gesture, had the desired effect and silenced her.

'One more dance,' Raúl said. 'Then I return you to Gordon.' He removed his finger. 'I'm sorry if you thought I was being rude—believe me, that was not my intention. Accept my apology, please.'

Estelle's eyes narrowed in suspicious assessment. She was aware of the pulse in her lips from his mere touch. Logic told her to remove herself from this situation, yet the stir of first arousal won.

The music slowed and, ignoring brief resistance, he pulled her in tighter. If she thought he was judging her, she was right—only it was not harshly. Raúl admired a woman who could separate emotion from sex.

Raúl needed exactly such a woman if he were to see this through.

He did not think her cheap: on the contrary, he intended to pay her very well.

She should have gone then—back to the table, to be ignored by the other guests. Should have left this man at a safer point. But her naïve body was refusing to walk away; instead it was awakening in his arms.

He held her so that her head was resting on his chest. She could feel the soft velvet of his jacket on her cheek. But she was more aware of his hand resting lightly on the base of her spine.

A couple dancing, each in a world of their own.

Raúl's motives were temporarily suspended. He enjoyed the soft weight that leant against him, the quiet of his mind as he focused only on her. The hand on her shoulder crept beneath her hair, his fingers lightly stroking the back of her neck, and again he wanted his mouth there, wanted to lift the raven curtain and taste her.

His fingers told her so—they stroked in a soft probing and they circled and teased as she swayed in time to the music. Estelle felt the stirring between them, and though her head denied what was happening her body shifted a little to allow for him. Her nipples hurt against his chest. His hand pressed her in just a little tighter as again he broke all boundaries. Again he voiced what perhaps others would not.

'I always thought a sporran was for decorative purposes only...'

She could feel the heat of its fur against her stomach.

'Yet it is the only thing keeping me decent.'

'You're *so* far from decent,' Estelle rasped.

'I know.'

They danced—not much, just swaying in time. Except she was on fire.

He could feel the heat of her skin on his fingers, could feel her breath so shallow that he wanted to lower his head and breathe into her mouth for her. He thought of her dark hair on his pillow, of her pink nipples in his mouth at the same time. He wanted her more than he had wanted any other, though Raúl was not comfortable with that thought.

This was business, Raúl reminded himself as motive returned. Tonight she would think of *his* lean, aroused body. When she was bedded by Gordon it would be *his* lithe body she ached for. He must now make sure of that. It was a business decision, and he made business decisions well.

His hand slid from beneath her hair down to the side of her ribs, to the bare skin there.

She ached. She ached for his hand to move, to cup her breast. And again he confirmed what was happening.

'Soon I return you to Gordon,' Raúl said, 'but first you come to *me*.'

It was foreplay. So much so she felt that as if his fingers were inside her. So much so that she could feel, despite the sporran, the thick outline beneath his kilt. It was the most dangerous dance of her life. She wanted to turn. She wanted to run. Except her body wanted the feel of his arms. Her burning cheeks rested against purple velvet and she could hear the steady thud of his heart as hers tripped and galloped. No one around them had a clue about the fire in his arms.

He smelt exquisite, and his cheek near hers had her head wanting to turn, to seek the relief of his mouth. She did not know the range of *la petit mort* or that he was giving her a mere taste. Estelle was far too innocent to know that she was building up to doing exactly as instructed and coming to him.

Raúl knew exactly when he felt the tension in his arms slowly abate, felt her slip a little down his chest as for a brief moment she relaxed against him.

'Thank you for the dance.' Breathless, stunned, she went to step back.

But still he held her as he lifted her chin and offered his verdict. 'You know, I would like to see you *really* cuss in Spanish.'

He let her go then, and Estelle headed to the safety of the ladies' room and ran her wrists under the tap to cool them.

Careful, she told herself. *Be careful here, Estelle.*

There was a blaze of attraction more intense than any she had known. What Estelle *did* know, though, was that a man like Raúl would crush her in the palm of his hand.

She looked up into the mirror and took out her lipstick; she could not fathom what had just taken place—nor that she had allowed it.

That she had partaken in it.

And willingly at that.

'There you are.'

Gordon smiled as she headed back to the table and she could not feel more guilty: she'd even failed as an escort.

'I'm so sorry to have left you—some foreign minister wanted to speak urgently with me, but we couldn't get him on the line and when we did…' Gordon gave a weary smile. 'He had no idea what he wanted to speak to me about. I've been going around in circles.' Gordon drained his drink. 'Let's dance.'

It felt very different dancing with Gordon. They laughed and chatted as she tried not to think about the dance with Raúl.

Yes, she danced with Gordon—but it was the black eyes still on her that held her mind. Raúl sat at the table drinking whisky.

'I think you've made quite an impression. Raúl can't keep his eyes off you.'

She started in his arms. 'It's okay, Estelle.' Gordon smiled. 'I'm flattered—or rather my persona is. To have Raúl as competition is a compliment indeed.'

He kissed her cheek and she rested her head on his shoulder, and then her eyes fell to Raúl's black eyes that still watched and there was heat in her body, and she tried to look away but she could not. She watched his mouth move in a slow smile till Gordon danced her so that Raúl was out of her line of vision. Then, a moment later, her eyes scanned the room for him and prayed that the dangerous part of her night was now over.

Raúl was gone.

CHAPTER SIX

'SORRY!'

Gordon apologised profusely for scaring her, after Estelle had walked into the guest room much later that night to find a monster!

He whipped the mask off. 'It's for my breathing. I have sleep apnoea.'

Estelle had changed in a tiny bathroom along the draughty hall and was now wearing some very old, very tatty pale pink pyjamas that she only put on when she was sick or reading for an entire weekend. It was all she'd had at short notice, but Estelle was quite sure Gordon wasn't expecting cleavage and sexy nightdresses.

She offered to take the sofa bed—he was paying her, after all—but true to his word he insisted that she have the bed.

'Thank you so much for tonight, Estelle.'

'It's been fine,' Estelle said as she rubbed cold cream into her face and took her make-up off. 'It must be so hard on you, though,' she mused, trying to get off the last of her mascara. 'Having to hide your real life.'

'It certainly hasn't been easy, but six months from now I'll be able to be myself.'

'Can't you now?'

'If it was just about me then I probably would have by

now,' Gordon explained. 'Frank is so private, though—it would be awful for him to have our relationship discussed on the news, which it would be. Still, six months from now we'll be sunning it in Spain.'

'Is that where you're going to live?'

'And marry,' Gordon said. 'Gay marriage is legal there.'

Estelle was really tired now; she slipped into bed and they chatted a little while more.

'You know that Virginia has nearly finished her studies…?'

'I know.' Estelle sighed—not only because she would miss her housemate, but also because she would need to find someone else to share if she continued with *her* course. But then she realised what Gordon was referring to.

'She's starting work next month. I don't want to offend you by suggesting anything, but if you did want to accompany me to things for a few months…'

He didn't push, and for that Estelle was grateful.

'Have a think about it,' Gordon said, and wished her goodnight.

Estelle was soon drifting off, thinking not about Gordon's offer but about Raúl and his pursuit.

And it *had* been a pursuit.

From the moment their eyes had locked he had barely left her thoughts or her side, whether standing behind her at the wedding or sitting beside her at dinner. She still could not comprehend what had taken place on the dance floor; she had been searching for the bells and whistles and sirens of an orgasm, but how delicious and gentle that had been—how much more was there to know?

She didn't dare think too much about it now. Exhausted from a long and tiring day, Estelle was just about to drift off to sleep when Gordon turned on his ventilation machine.

Ginny hadn't told her about this part.

She lay there, head under pillow, at two a.m., still listening to the CPAP machine whirring and hissing. In the end she gave in.

She padded through the castle, her bare feet making not a sound on the stone floor. She headed to the small bathroom and took a drink from the tap, willing the night to be over.

Then she looked at her surroundings and regretted willing it over.

She stepped out onto a huge stone balcony, stared out to the loch. It was incredibly light for this time of the morning. She breathed in the warm summer night air and now her thoughts *did* turn to Gordon and his offer.

Estelle had already been coming to a reluctant decision to defer her studies and work full-time. It was all so big and scary—a future that was unknown.

She turned as the door opened, her eyes widening as Raúl stepped out.

He was wearing only his kilt.

Estelle would have preferred him with clothes on. Not because there was anything to disappoint—far from it—but the sight of olive skin, the light fan of hair on his chest and the way the kilt hung gave her eyes just one place to linger. There was nothing safe about meeting his gaze.

It was only then that she realised he had not followed her out here—that instead he was speaking on the phone.

He must have come out to get better reception. She gave him a brief smile and went to brush past, to get away from him without incident, but his hand caught her wrist and she stood there as he spoke into the phone.

'You don't need to know what room I am in...' He rolled his eyes. 'Araminta, I suggest that you go to bed.' He let out an irritated hiss. 'Alone!'

He ended the call and only then dropped Estelle's wrist. She stood as he examined her face.

'You know, without all the make-up you slather on…' His eyes searched her unmade-up skin. Her hair was tied in a low ponytail and she was dressed in a way he would not expect Gordon to find pleasing.

Raúl did.

She looked young—so much younger without all the make-up—and her baggy pyjamas left it all to Raúl's imagination. Which he was using now.

And then came his verdict.

'You look stunning,' Raúl said. 'I'm surprised Gordon has let you out of his sight.'

'I just needed some air.'

'I am hiding,' Raúl admitted.

'From Araminta?'

'Someone must have given her my phone number. I am going to have to change it.'

'She'll give in soon.' Estelle smiled, feeling a little sorry for the other woman. If Araminta had had a fling with him a few years ago and had known he would be here tonight—well, Estelle could see why her hopes might have been raised.

His phone rang again and he rolled his eyes and chose not to answer. 'So, what are you doing out here at this time of morning?'

'Just thinking.'

'About what?'

'Things.' She gave a wry smile, didn't add that far too many of her thoughts had been about him.

'And me,' Raúl admitted. 'It has been an interesting day.'

He looked out to the still, silent loch and felt a world away from where he had woken this morning. He didn't even know how he was feeling. He looked over to Estelle, who was gazing out into the night too, a woman who was comfortable with silence.

It was Raúl who was not—Raúl who made sure his days and nights were always filled to capacity so that exhaustion could claim him each night.

Here, for the first time in the longest time, he found himself alone with his thoughts—and that was not pleasant. But he refused to pick up to Araminta, knowing the chaos that might create.

It was Raúl who broke the silence. He wanted to hear her voice.

'When do you go back?'

'Late morning.' Estelle stared out ahead. 'You?'

'I will leave early.'

He walked to lean over the balcony, gazed into the night, and Estelle saw the huge scar that ran from his shoulder to his waist. He glanced around and saw the slight shock on her face. Usually he refused to offer an explanation for the scar—he did not need sympathy. Tonight he chose to explain it.

'It's from the car accident...'

'That killed your mother?'

He gave a curt nod and turned back to look into the night, breathing in the cool air. He was glad that she was here. For no other reason, Raúl realised, than he was glad. It was two a.m. in the second longest night of his life, and for the first one he had been alone.

'Can I ask again?' He had to know. 'What are you doing with Gordon?'

'He's nice.'

'So are many people. It doesn't mean we go around...' He did not complete his sentence yet he'd made his rather crude point. 'Are you here tonight for your brother?'

Estelle could not answer. She had agreed to be here for Gordon, yet she knew they both knew the truth.

'Do you have siblings?' Estelle asked.

There was a long stretch of silence. His father had asked that he not reveal anything just yet, but it would all be out in the open soon. Estelle came and stood beside him as she awaited his answer. Perhaps she would go straight to the press in the morning. Raúl actually did not care right now. He could not think about tomorrow. It was taking all his control to get through the night.

'Had you asked me that yesterday the answer would have been no.' He turned his head, saw her frown at his answer and was grateful that she did not push for more detail. Instead she stayed silent as Raúl admitted a little of the truth. 'This morning my father told me that I have a brother—Luka.' It felt strange to say his name. 'Luka Sanchez Garcia.'

From their little lesson earlier, Estelle knew they did not share the same mother. 'Have you met him?'

'Unwittingly.'

'How old is he?'

She asked the same question that he had asked his father, though the relevance of the answer she could not know.

'Twenty-five,' Raúl said. 'I walked into my father's office this morning, expecting my usual lecture—he insists it is time for me to settle down.' He gave a small mirthless laugh. 'I had no idea what was coming. My father is dying and he wants his affairs put in order. My affairs too. And so he told me he has another son...'

'It must have been the most terrible shock.'

'Skeletons in the closet are not unique,' Raúl said. 'But this was not some long-ago affair that has suddenly come to light. My father has kept another life. He sees his mistress in the north of Spain. I thought he went there so regularly for work. We have a hotel in San Sebastian. It is his main interest. Now I know why.'

Estelle tried to imagine what it was like, finding out something like this, and Raúl stood trying to comprehend that he had actually told another—how readily he had opened up to her. Then he reminded himself why. For his solution to come to fruition of *course* Estelle had to be told.

Some of it, at least.

He would never reveal all.

'His PA—Angela—she has always been…'

He gave a tight shrug. Angela had not been so much like a mother, but she had been a constant—a woman he trusted. Raúl closed his eyes, remembered walking out of his father's office and the words he had hurled to the one woman he had believed did not have an agenda.

'We have always got on. It turns out the son she speaks of often is in fact my half-brother.' He gave a wry smile. 'A lot of my childhood was spent with my aunt or uncle. I assumed my father was working at the hotel in San Sebastian. It turns out he was with his mistress and his son.' Black was the hiss that came from his mouth. 'It's all sorry and excuses now. I always prided myself on knowing what goes on, on being astute. It turns out I knew nothing.'

He had said enough. More than enough for one night.

'So, in answer to your question—yes. I have a brother.'

He shrugged naked shoulders and her fingers balled into her palms in an effort not to rest her hand on them.

'Unlike you, I care nothing for mine.'

'You might if you knew him.'

'That's not going to happen.'

She felt a small shiver, put it down to the night air. But his voice was so black with loathing it could have been that. 'I'm going to go in.'

'Please don't.'

Estelle had to get back—back to the safety of Gordon—yet she did not want to walk away from him.

She had to.

'Goodnight, Raúl...'

'Stay.'

She shook her head, grateful for the ringing of his phone—for the diversion it offered. But as she went to open the door she heard a woman's frantic voice coming down the corridor.

'Pick up Raúl. Where the hell are you?'

He had lightning reflexes. Quickly Raúl turned his phone off and pulled Estelle into the shadows.

'I need a favour.'

Before she knew what was happening she was in his arms, his tongue prising her lips open, his hand at her pyjama top. Estelle struggled against him before realising what was happening. She could hear Araminta calling out to Raúl, and if she saw the balcony any moment now she would come out.

But Araminta didn't. She stumbled past the balcony, the couple on it unseen.

He could stop now, Estelle thought. Except her pyjama top was completely open, her breasts splayed against his naked chest.

We *should* stop now, she thought as his tongue chased hers.

He made a low moan into her mouth; it was the sexiest thing she had ever heard or felt. He slid one hand over her bottom and his tongue was hot and moist.

Suddenly sending a message to Araminta was the last thing on Raúl's mind.

Estelle wanted his kiss to end, and yet she yearned for it to go on—like a forbidden path she was running down, wanting to get to the end, to glimpse again the woman he made her. It was a kiss that should not be happening, but it was one she did not want to end.

'Don't go back to him...' Raúl's mouth barely left hers as he voiced his command.

He had intended to speak with her at a later point, perhaps get her phone number, but having tasted her, having kissed her, he could not stand the thought of her in Gordon's bed. He would reveal his plan right now.

He peeled his mouth off hers, his breath coming hard on her lips. 'Come now with me.'

It was then that she fully realised her predicament. Raúl assumed this was the norm for her, that she readily gave her body.

As he moved in to kiss her again she slapped him. It was the only way she knew how to end this.

'You pay more, do you?' She was disgusted with his thought processes.

'I did not mean it like that.' Raúl felt the sting on his cheek and knew that it was merited—knew how his suggestion must have come across. But business had been the last thing on his mind. He had simply not wanted her going back to another man. 'I meant—'

'I know exactly what you meant.'

'Bastard!'

They both turned at the sight of a tear-streaked Araminta. 'You said you were tired, that you were in bed.'

'Can I suggest that you go back to your bed?' Raúl snapped to Araminta, clearly not welcoming the intrusion.

Estelle saw again just how brutal this man could be when he chose.

'How much clearer can I make it that I have absolutely no interest in you?'

He turned and came to help a mortified Estelle with her buttons, but her hand slapped him off.

'Don't touch me!'

She flew from the balcony and back to her room, stepped quietly in and slipped into bed, listened to the whirring of Gordon's machine, trying to forget the feel of Raúl's hands, his mouth.

Trying to deny that she lay there for the first time truly wanting.

CHAPTER SEVEN

'ESTELLE…'

Gordon was lovely when she told him what had happened. Well, not all of it. She didn't tell him about her conversation with Raúl, just that he had been trying to avoid a woman and had kissed her…

It was a terribly awkward conversation, but Gordon was writing her a cheque, so as not to embarrass her in front of his driver, and Estelle simply couldn't accept it and had to tell him why.

'Frank and I have three free passes.'

Estelle blinked as Gordon smiled and held out the cheque.

'We have three people each who, should something happen, wouldn't be construed as cheating with.' He gave her a smile. 'It's just a game, of course, and it's mainly movie stars, but Raúl could very easily make it to my list. No one can resist him when he sets his sights on them—especially someone as darling and innocent as you.'

'I feel awful.'

'Don't.' Gordon closed her hand around the cheque. 'My being in competition with Raúl Sanchez Fuente could only do wonders for my reputation, if word were ever to get out. It might even be the reason for our breaking up and me realising just how much I care for Virginia.'

'I'm sorry.'

'Don't be,' Gordon said, and gave her a kiss on the cheek. 'Just be careful.'

'I'll never see him again,' Estelle said. 'He doesn't know anything about me.'

'Mere details to a man like Raúl—and he takes care of them easily.'

Estelle felt the hairs on her arms stand up as she remembered that she had given him her name.

'Just do your hair and put on a ton of make-up and we'll head down for breakfast,' Gordon told her. 'If anyone says anything about last night just laugh and shrug it off.'

It was a relief to hide her blushes behind thick make-up. Estelle put on a skirt that was too short and some high wedges, and tied her hair in a high ponytail and then teased it with a comb and sprayed it.

'I feel like a clown,' she said to Gordon as she checked her reflection in the mirror.

'Well, you make *me* smile.'

Raúl had gone, and all Estelle had to endure were some daggers being thrown in her direction by Araminta as they ate a full Scottish breakfast. She was relieved not to see him, yet there was a curious disappointment at his absence which Estelle chose not to examine.

Finally they were on their way, but it was late afternoon before Gordon dropped her at her home.

'Think about what I said,' Gordon reminded Estelle as she climbed out.

'I think I've had my excitement for the year,' Estelle admitted as she farewelled him.

She let herself step into familiar surrounds and released a breath before calling out to Ginny that she was home.

'How are you feeling?' Estelle asked as she walked into the lounge.

'Awful!'

Ginny certainly looked it.

'I'm going to go home for a couple of days. My dad's coming to pick me up—I need Mum, soup and sympathy.'

'Sounds good.'

'How was it?

'It was fine,' Estelle said, really not in the mood to tell Ginny all that had happened.

Ginny would no doubt find out from Gordon, given how much the two of them discussed. Estelle was still irritated that Ginny told Gordon about her virginity but, seeing how sick Ginny was, Estelle chose to save that for later.

'Gordon was lovely.'

'I told you there was nothing to worry about.'

'I'm exhausted,' Estelle admitted. 'You didn't tell me about Gordon's sleep apnoea. I got the fright of my life when I walked in and he was strapped to a machine.'

Ginny laughed. 'I honestly forgot. Your brother's been calling you. A few times, actually.'

The phone rang then, and Estelle's heart lurched in hope when she saw that it was her brother. 'Maybe he's got that job.'

He hadn't.

'I found out on Friday,' Andrew said. 'I just couldn't face telling you.'

'Something will come up.'

'I'm not qualified for anything.'

Estelle could hear the hopelessness in his voice.

'I don't know what to do, Estelle. I've asked Amanda's parents if they can help—'

His voice broke then. Estelle knew the hell that would have paid with his pride.

'They can't.'

She could feel his mounting despair.

'Something will come up,' Estelle said, but she was finding it harder and harder to sound convincing. 'You've just got to keep applying for work.'

'I know.' He blew out a long breath in an effort to compose himself. 'Anyway, enough about me,' Andrew said, 'Ginny said you were in Scotland. How come?'

'I was at a wedding.'

'Whose?'

'I'll tell you all about it tomorrow.'

'Tomorrow?'

'I want to speak to you about something.' As a car tooted outside, Ginny stood. 'Andrew, I've got to go,' Estelle said. 'I'll call in tomorrow.'

Estelle didn't know how to tell Andrew she had some money for him, but anyway she knew that one month's mortgage payment would only be a Band-Aid solution. She was relieved that Ginny would be out for a few days because she really wanted some time to go over what she was considering.

The library was offering her more hours. Perhaps she could defer her studies and move in with Andrew and Amanda for a year, pay them rent, help out with little Cecelia, maybe even take Gordon up on his offer... Yes, she was glad Ginny would be away, because she needed to think properly.

'Your dad's here,' Estelle said.

'Thanks so much for last night, Estelle,' Ginny said, grabbing her bag and heading out of the door, waving to her father, who had climbed back into the car when he saw her.

Ginny was too dosed up on flu medication even to notice the expensive car a little further down the road.

Raúl noticed *her*, though—and a frown appeared on his face as he saw Virginia, Gordon's regular date, disappearing into a car driven by another older male. After Raúl's father's revelations he was past being surprised by anything, but there was a curious feeling of disappointment as he thought of Estelle and Virginia together with Gordon.

No.

He did not like the images that conjured, so he settled for the slightly more palatable version—that Estelle hadn't picked him up at Dario's; instead Estelle and Virginia must both work for the same escort agency.

He needed someone tough, Raúl told himself. He needed a woman who could separate sex from emotion, who could see what he was about to propose as a financial opportunity rather than a romantic proposition.

Except his knuckles were white as he clutched the steering wheel. Since last night there had been an incessant gnawing in his stomach when he thought of Estelle with Gordon. Now that gnawing had upgraded to a burn in the lining of his gut.

Estelle would be far better with him.

Was he arrogant to think so? Raúl pondered briefly as he walked up her garden path.

Perhaps, he conceded, but he was also assured enough to know that he was right.

'What did you forget…?' Estelle's voice trailed off when she saw that it wasn't Ginny.

Raúl preferred the way she'd looked last night on the balcony, but her appearance now—the short skirt, the heavy make-up, the lacquered hair—actually made things easier.

'What do you want?'

'I wanted to apologise for what I said last night. I think it was misconstrued.'

'I think you made things perfectly clear.' She drew in

a breath and then gave a small nod. 'Apology accepted. Now, if you'll excuse me?'

Her hand was ready to close the door on him. There was just a moment and Raúl knew he had to use it wisely. There was no time for mixed messages. He knew he had better reveal the truth up-front.

'You were right—I didn't want you to go back to Gordon, but not just because...' The door was closing on him so Raúl told her exactly what he was here for. 'I wanted to ask you to marry me.'

Estelle laughed.

After the tension of the last twenty-four hours, then her brother's tears on the phone, and now Raúl, standing absolutely immaculate in black jeans and a shirt at her door with his ridiculous proposal, all she could do was throw her head back and laugh.

'I'm serious.'

'Of course you are,' Estelle answered. 'Just as you were serious last night when you told me just how much you don't want to marry—ever.'

'I don't want to marry for love,' Raúl said, 'but I do need a bride. One with a level head. One who knows what she wants and goes for it.'

There was that implication again, Estelle realised. She was about to close the door, but then she looked down to the cheque Raul was holding—one with her name on it—and she saw the ridiculous amount he was offering. He surely wasn't serious. She looked up at him and realised that possibly he was—that he could pay for her services. As Gordon had.

Estelle gave a nervous swallow, reminding herself that whatever happened, whatever Raúl thought, she must not betray Gordon's confidence.

'Look—whatever you think, Gordon and I...'

'Should that be, Gordon, *Virginia* and I?' He watched her flaming cheeks pale. 'I just saw her leave. Are you both dating him?'

'I don't have to explain anything to you.'

'You're right,' Raúl conceded.

'How did you know where I lived?'

'I checked your bag when you were dancing with Gordon.'

Estelle blinked. He was honest, brutally honest—and, yes, she couldn't help herself. She was curious.

'Are you going to ask me in or do I stand and speak here?'

'I don't think so.' Common sense told her to close the door on him, but as she stared into black eyes curiosity was starting to win. Things like this—conversations like this—simply didn't happen to Estelle. But, more than that, she wanted to find out more about this man who had been on her mind from the second their eyes had locked.

'I ask for ten minutes,' Raúl said. 'If you want me to leave then, I shall, and I will never bother you again.'

He spoke in such a matter-of-fact voice. This was business to him, Estelle realised, and he assumed it was the same for her. She chose to keep it that way.

'Ten minutes,' Estelle said, and opened the door.

He looked around the small house. It was typical student accommodation, yet she was not your typical student.

'You are studying?'

'Yes.'

'Can I ask what?'

Estelle hesitated, not keen on revealing anything to him, but surely it could do no harm. 'Ancient architecture.'

'Really?' Raul frowned. Her response was not the one he'd been expecting.

She offered him a seat and Raúl took it. Estelle chose a

chair on the opposite side of the room to him. He wasted no time getting to the point.

'I have told you that my father is sick?' Raúl said, and Estelle nodded. 'And that for a long time he has wanted to see me settled? Now, with his death nearing, more and more he wishes to see his wish fulfilled—he has convinced himself that a wife will tame my ways.'

Estelle said nothing. She just looked at this man she doubted would ever be tamed; she had tasted his passion, had heard about his appalling reputation. A ring on his finger certainly wouldn't have stopped what had taken place last night.

'You might remember I told you my father revealed he has another son?'

Again Estelle nodded.

'He has said that if I do not comply, if I do not settle down, then he will leave his share of the business to my...' He could not bring himself to call Luka his brother. 'I refuse to allow that to happen.'

She could see the determination in his eyes.

'Which is why I have come this evening to speak with you.'

'Why aren't you having this conversation with Araminta? I'm sure she'd be delighted to marry you.'

'I did briefly consider it,' Raúl admitted, 'but there are several reasons. The main one being she would not be able to reconcile the fact that this is a business transaction. She would agree, I think, but it would be with hope that love would grow, that perhaps a baby might change my mind. It will not,' Raúl said. His voice was definite. 'Which is why I come to speak with you. A woman who understands a certain business.'

'I really think you have the wrong idea about me.'

'I am not here to judge you. On the contrary, I admire a woman who can separate love from sex.'

He did not understand the wry smile on her face. If only he knew. It faded as he continued.

'We are attracted to each other.' Raúl said it as a fact. 'Surely for you that can only be a bonus?'

Estelle blew out a breath; he was practically calling her a hooker and yet she was in a poor position to deny it.

'We both like to party,' Raúl said. 'And we like to live life in the fast lane—even if we know how to take things seriously at times.'

He was wrong about the fast lane, and Estelle knew if she admitted the truth he'd be gone. But, yes, she *was* undeniably attracted to him. Her skin was tingling just from his presence. Her mind was still begging for a moment of peace just to process the dance and the kiss they had shared last night.

He interrupted her wandering thoughts.

'Estelle. I have spoken with my father's doctor; it is a matter of weeks rather than months. You would only be away for a short while.'

'Away?'

'I live in Marbella.'

Now she definitely shook her head. 'Raúl, I have a life here. My niece is sick. I am studying…'

'You can return to your studies a wealthy woman—and naturally you will have regular trips home.'

He looked at her, with her gaudy make-up and teased hair. He chose to remember her fresh-faced on the balcony, recalled the comfort she had given even before they had kissed. He should not care, but he did not like the life she was leading. Suddenly it was imperative for reasons other than appeasing his father that she take this chance.

'I do not judge you, Estelle, but you could come back

and start over. You can live the life you want to without ever having to worry about the rent.'

Estelle stood and walked to the window, not wanting him to see the tears that sprang in her eyes because for a moment there he had sounded as if he actually cared.

'You certainly won't have to host dinner parties or cook for me. I work hard all day. You can shop. We'll eat out every night. And there are many clubs to choose from, parties to attend. You would never be bored.'

He had no idea about her at all.

'After my father's death, after a suitable pause, we will admit our whirlwind marriage cannot deal with the grief— that with regret we are to part. No one will ever know you married for money. That would be written into the contract.'

'Contract?'

'Of course,' Raúl said. 'One that will protect both of us, that will lay down all the rules. I have asked my lawyer to fly in for a meeting at midday tomorrow. Naturally it will be a lengthy meeting. We will have to go over terms.'

'I won't be there.'

He didn't look in the least deterred.

'Raúl, my brother would never believe me.'

'I will come with you and speak to him.'

'Oh, and he'll believe *you*? He'll believe we met yester-day and fell madly in love? He'll have me certified insane before he lets me fly off with a stranger—'

'We met last year.' Raúl interrupted her tirade. It was clear he had thought it all through. 'When you were in Spain. It was then that we fell madly in love, but of course with your brother's accident it was not the time to say so, or to make plans to move, so we put it down to a holiday romance. We met again a few weeks ago and this time around I had no intention of letting you go.'

'I don't want to lie to him.'

'You are always truthful?' Raúl checked. 'Does he know about Gordon, then? Does he know—?'

'Okay,' she interrupted. Because of course there were things her brother didn't know. She was actually considering it—so much so that she turned to him with a question. 'Would *your* family believe it?'

'Before I found out about my father's other life I chose to let him think I was serious about someone I used to date. It was not you I had in mind, but they do not know that.'

It could work.

The frown that was on her brow was smoothed, the impossibility of it all was fading, and Raúl knew it was time to leave.

'Sleep on it,' Raúl said. 'Naturally there is more that I have to tell you, but I am not prepared to discuss certain things until after the marriage.'

'What sort of things?'

'Nothing that impacts on you now—just things that a loving wife would know all about. It is something I would not reveal to anyone I did not trust or love.'

'Or pay for?'

'Yes.' He placed the cheque on the coffee table and handed her two business cards.

'That is the hotel my lawyer will be staying at. I have booked an office there. The other card contains my contact details—for now.'

'For now?'

'I am changing my phone number tomorrow,' Raúl said. 'One other thing…' He ran a finger along her cheek, looked at the full mouth he had so enjoyed kissing last night. 'There will be no one else for the duration of our contract…'

'It's not going to happen.'

'Well, in case you change your mind—' he handed her an envelope '—you might need this.'

She opened it, stared at the photo that had been taken last night. His arm was on the chair behind her, she was laughing, and there was Raúl—smiling, absolutely beautiful, his eyes on her, staring at her as if he was entranced.

He must have known the photographer was on his way, Estelle realised. He had been considering this even last night.

Raúl *had* rearranged the seating—she was certain of it now.

She realised then the lengths he would go to to get his way.

'Did you arrange for Gordon to be called away?'

'Of course.'

'You don't even try to deny it?'

He heard her anger.

'You'd prefer that I lie?' Raúl checked.

She looked to the mantelpiece, to the photo of her brother and Amanda holding a tiny, frail Cecelia. She was so tired of struggling. But she could not believe that she was considering his offer. She had considered Gordon's, though, Estelle told herself. Tomorrow she had been going to tell her brother she was deferring her studies and moving in with them.

She had already made the decision to up-end her life.

This would certainly up-end it—but in a rather more spectacular way.

She went into the kitchen with the excuse of making coffee, but really it was to gather her thoughts.

Bought by Raúl.

Estelle closed her eyes. It was against everything she believed in, yet it wasn't just the money that tempted her. It was something more base than that.

A man as beautiful as Raúl, for her first lover. The thought of sharing his bed, his life—even for a little while—was as tempting as the cheque he had written. Estelle blew out a breath, her skin on fire, aroused just at the thought of lying beside him. Yet she knew that if Raúl knew she was a virgin the deal would be off.

'Not for me.'

He was standing at the kitchen door, watching as she spooned instant coffee into two mugs.

'I'll leave you to think about it. If you do not arrive at the appointment then I will accept your decision and stop the cheque. As I said, tomorrow my phone number will be changing. It will be too late to change your mind.'

It really was, Estelle knew, a once-in-a-lifetime offer.

CHAPTER EIGHT

'I WILL FLY your family out for the wedding...'

They were sitting in Raúl's lawyer's office, going over details that made Estelle burn, but it was all being dealt with in a cool, precise manner.

'I will speak with your parents and brother.'

'My parents are both deceased.' Estelle said it in a matter-of-fact way. She was not after sympathy from Raúl and this was not a tender conversation. 'And my brother and his wife won't be able to attend—Cecelia is too sick to travel.'

'You should have *someone* there for you.'

'Won't your family believe us otherwise?' There was a slight sneer to her voice, which she fought to check. She had chosen to be here, after all. It was just the mention of her parents, of Cecelia, that had her throat tightening— the realisation that everything in this marriage bar love would be real and she would be going through it all alone.

'It has nothing to do with that,' Raúl said. 'It is your wedding day. You might find it overwhelming to be alone.'

'Oh, please,' Estelle responded, determined not to let him see her fear. 'I'll be fine.'

'Very well.' Raúl nodded. 'It will be a small wedding, but traditional. The press will go wild—they have been waiting a long time for me to marry—but we will not let them know we are married till after.'

They had been talking for hours; every detail from wardrobe allowance to hair and make-up had been discussed.

Estelle had insisted she could choose her own clothes.

'I have a reputation to think of,' had been Raúl's tart response.

Estelle was entitled to one week every month to come back to the UK and visit her family for the duration of the contract.

'I am sure we will both need the space,' had been Raúl's explanation. 'I am not used to having someone permanently around.'

There was now an extremely uncomfortable conversation—for Estelle, in any case—about the regularity of sex, and also about birth control and health checks. Raúl didn't appear in the least bit fazed.

'In the event of a pregnancy—' the lawyer started.

Raúl was quick to interrupt. Only now did he seem concerned by the subject matter being discussed. 'There is to be no pregnancy.' There was a low menace to his voice. 'I don't think my bride-to-be would be foolish enough to try and trap me in *that* way.'

'It still needs to be addressed.' The lawyer was very calm.

'I have no intention of getting pregnant.' Estelle gave a small nervous laugh, truly horrified at the prospect. She had seen the stress Cecelia had placed on Andrew and Amanda, and they were head over heels in love.

'You might change your mind,' Raúl said, for he trusted no one. 'You might decide that you like the lifestyle and don't want to give it up.' He looked to his lawyer. 'We need to make contingency plans.'

'Absolutely,' the lawyer said.

It could not be made clearer that this was all business.

Estelle sat as with clinical detachment he ensured that he would provide for any child they might have on the condition that the child resided in Spain.

If she moved back to England, Estelle would have to fight against his might just to make the rent.

'I think that covers it,' the lawyer said.

'Not quite.' Estelle cleared her throat. 'I'd like us to agree that we won't sleep with each other till after the wedding.'

'There's no need for quaint.'

'I've agreed to all your terms.' She looked coolly at him. It was the only way for this to work. If he knew she was a virgin this meeting would close now. 'You can surely agree to one of mine? I'd like some time off before I start *working*.' She watched his jaw tighten slightly as she made it clear that this *was* work.

'Very well.' Raúl did not like to be told that sleeping with him would be a chore. 'You may well change your mind.'

'I shan't.'

'You will be flown in a couple of days before the wedding. I will be on my yacht, partying as grooms do before their marriage. You shall have the apartment to yourself.' He had no intention of holding hands and playing coy for a week. He waited for her nod and then turned to his lawyer. 'Draft it.'

They waited in a sumptuous lounge as the lawyer got to work, but Estelle couldn't relax.

'You are tense.'

'It's not every day you get offered a million dollars.' She could at least be honest about that. 'Nor move to Marbella...'

'You will love it,' Raúl said. 'The night-life is fantastic…'

He just didn't know her at all, Estelle realised yet again.

'How did your parents die?' Raúl asked, watching as her shoulders stiffened. 'My family are bound to ask.'

'In a car accident,' Estelle said, turning to him. 'The same as your mother.'

He opened his mouth to speak and then changed his mind.

'I just hope everyone believes us,' Estelle said.

'Why wouldn't they? Even when we divorce we'll maintain the lie. You understand the confidentiality clause?' Raúl checked. 'No one is ever to know that this is a marriage of convenience only.'

'No one will ever hear it from me,' she assured him. The prospect of being found out was abhorrent to Estelle. 'Just a whirlwind romance and a marriage that didn't work out.'

'Good,' Raúl said. 'And, Estelle—even if we do get on…even if you do like—'

'Don't worry, Raúl,' she interrupted. 'I'm not going to be falling in love with you.' She gave him a tight smile. 'I'll be out of your life, as per the contract.'

CHAPTER NINE

RAÚL HAD BEEN RIGHT.

Estelle stood on the balcony of his luxurious apartment, looking out at the marina, on the morning of her wedding day, and was, as Raúl had predicted, utterly and completely overwhelmed.

She had arrived in Marbella two days ago and had barely stopped for air since. Stepping into this vast apartment, she had fully glimpsed his wealth. Every room bar the movie screening room was angled to take in the stunning view of the Mediterranean, and every whim was catered for from Jacuzzi to sauna. There was a whole new wardrobe waiting for her too. The only thing lacking was that the kitchen cupboards and fridge were empty.

'Call Sol's if you don't want to go out,' Raúl had said. 'They will bring whatever you want straight over.'

The only vaguely familiar thing had been the photo of them both, taken at Donald's wedding, beautifully framed and on a wall. But even that had been dealt with by Raúl. It had been manipulated so that her make-up was softer, her cleavage less revealing.

It had been a sharp reminder that he thought her a tart.

Raúl knew the woman he wanted to marry, and it wasn't the woman he had met, so there had been trips to a beauty salon for hair treatments and make-up lessons.

'I don't *need* make-up lessons,' Estelle had said.

'Oh, baby, you do,' had been his response. 'Subtle is best.'

Constantly she had to remind herself to be the woman he thought he had met. A woman who acted as if delighted by her new designer wardrobe, who didn't mind at all when he told her to wear factor fifty-plus because he liked her pale skin.

But it wasn't that which concerned Estelle this morning as she looked out at the glittering sea and the luxurious yachts, wondering which one was Raúl's.

Tonight she would be on his yacht.

This night they would be sharing a bed.

Estelle wasn't sure if she was more terrified of losing her virginity, or of him finding out that she had never slept with anyone before.

Maybe he wouldn't notice, she thought helplessly. But she knew she didn't have a hope of delivering to his bed the sexually experienced woman that Raúl was expecting. Last night, before heading off with his sponsors for his final night as a single man, Raúl had kissed her slowly and deeply. The message his tongue had delivered had been an explicit one.

'Why do you make me wait?'

Tonight he would find out why.

'You have a phone call.' Rosa, his housekeeper, brought the phone up to the balcony. It was Amanda on the line.

'How are you doing?' Amanda asked.

'I'm petrified.' It was nice to be honest.

'All brides are,' Amanda said. 'But Raúl will take good care of you.'

He had utterly and completely charmed Amanda, but had not quite won over Andrew.

'I am not letting her go again.' He had looked Andrew

straight in the eye as he said it. 'If I move Estelle to Spain I want to make a proper commitment. That is why she will come to be my wife.'

So easily he had lied.

Estelle knew she must remember that fact.

'How did the dress turn out?' Amanda asked.

'It's beautiful,' Estelle said. 'Even better than I imagined it would be.'

It was the only thing Estelle had been allowed to organise. It had all be done online and by phone, and the final adjustments made when she had arrived.

'How is Cecelia?' Estelle asked, desperate for news of her niece.

'She's still asleep.'

It was nine a.m. in Spain, which meant it was eight a.m. in the UK. Cecelia had always been an early riser. More and more she slept these days, though Amanda always did her best to be upbeat.

'I'm going to dress her up for the wedding and take a photo and send it. Even if we can't be there today, know that we're thinking of you.'

'I know.'

'And I'm not your sister, but I do think of you as one.'

'Thank you,' Estelle said, her eyes welling up. 'I think of you as a sister too.'

They weren't idle words; many hours had been spent in hospital waiting rooms this past year.

'Is that the door?' Amanda asked.

'Yes. Don't worry, someone else will get it.'

'Do you have a butler?'

'No!' Estelle laughed, swallowing down her tears. 'Just Raúl's housekeeper. Though it's going to start to get busy soon, with the hairdresser...' She turned around as she heard her name being called, and Estelle's jaw dropped as she saw her brother coming through the door.

'Andrew!'

'Is that where he's got to?' Amanda laughed, and then she was serious. 'I'm so sorry that I couldn't be with you today—I'd have given anything. But with Cecelia...'

'Thank you,' Estelle said, and promptly burst into tears, all her pent-up nerves released.

'I think she's pleased to see me,' Andrew said, taking the phone and chatting to Amanda briefly before hanging up.

'I can't believe you're here,' Estelle admitted.

'Raúl said he thought you might need someone today, and of course I wanted to give you away. If anything happens with Cecelia he's assured me I'll be able to get straight back.'

She couldn't believe that Raúl would do this for her. Until now she hadn't fully realised how terrifying today was, how real it felt.

Raúl had.

'When did you get in?'

'Last night,' Andrew said. 'We went to Sol's.'

'You were out with Raúl?'

'He certainly knows how to party.' Andrew smiled. 'I'd forgotten how.'

Even if she was doing all this for her brother and his wife, of the many benefits of marrying Raúl, this was one Estelle had not even considered—that her brother, who was still having trouble accepting the diagnosis that he would never walk again, who had, apart from job interviews and hospital appointments, become almost reclusive, would fly not just to Spain but so far out of his comfort zone.

It was a huge and important step, and it was thanks to Raúl that he was here.

'I've got something for you.'

Estelle bit her lip, hoping they hadn't spent money they didn't have on a gift for a wedding that wasn't real.

'Remember these?' Andrew said as she opened the box. 'These' were small diamond studs that had belonged to her mother. 'Dad bought them for her for their wedding day.'

She had never felt more of a fraud.

'Enough tears,' Andrew said. 'Let's get this wedding underway.'

Raúl was rarely nervous, but as he stood at the altar and waited for Estelle, to his own surprise, he was.

His father had almost bought their story, and Raul's future with the company was secure, but instead of a gloating satisfaction that his plans were falling into place today he thought only of the reasons he had had to go to these lengths.

His head turned briefly and he caught a glimpse of Angela in the middle of the church. She was seated with his father, as ever-present PA. His mother's family were still unaware of the real role she played in his father's life—and the role she had played in his mother's death.

He stared ahead, anger churning in his gut that Angela had the gall to be here. He wouldn't put it past her to bring her bastard son.

Then he heard the murmur of the congregation and Raúl turned around. The churning faded. Just one thought was now in his mind.

She looked beautiful.

He had wondered how Estelle might look—had worried that, left to her own devices, a powder-puff ball would be wobbling towards him on glittery platform shoes, smiling from ruby-red lips.

He had not—could not have—imagined this.

Her dress was cream and made of intricate Spanish lace. It was fitted, and showing her curves, but in the most elegant of ways. The neckline was a simple halter neck. She carried orange blossom, as was the tradition for Spanish brides, and her lipstick was a pale coral.

'Te ves bella.' He told her that she looked beautiful as she joined him, and he meant every word. Not one thing would he change, from her black hair, piled high up on her head, to the simple diamond earrings and elegant cream shoes. She was visibly shaking, and he made a small joke to relax her. 'Your sewing is terrible.'

She glanced at his shirt and they shared a smile. With so little history, still they found a piece now, at the altar—as per tradition, the bride-to-be must embroider her groom's shirt.

'I'm not marrying a billionaire to sit sewing!' she had said teasingly, and Raúl had laughed, explaining that most women did not embroider all of the front of the shirt these days. Only a small area would be left for her, and Estelle could put on it whatever she wanted.

He had half expected a € but had frowned this morning when he had put on his shirt to find a small pineapple. Raúl still couldn't work out what it meant, but it was nice to see her relax and smile as the service started.

They knelt together, and as the service moved along he explained things in his low, deep voice, heard only by her.

'El lazo,' he said as a loop of satin decorated with orange blossom was placed over his shoulders and then another loop from the same piece was placed over hers. The priest spoke then for a moment, in broken English, and Estelle's cheeks burnt red as he told them that the rope that bound them showed that they shared the responsibility for this marriage. It would remain for the rest of the ceremony.

But not for life.

She felt like a fraud. She *was* a fraud, Estelle thought, panic starting to build. But Raúl took her hand and she looked into his black eyes. He seemed to sense that she was suddenly struggling.

'He asks now that you hand him the Arras,' Raúl said and she handed over the small purse he had given her on arrival. It contained thirteen coins, he had explained, and it showed his financial commitment to her.

It was the only honest part of the service, Estelle thought as the priest blessed them and handed it back to her.

Except it felt real.

'It's okay,' he said to her. 'We are here in this together.'

It felt far safer than being in it alone.

The service ended and an attendant removed the satin rope and presented it to Estelle; then they walked out to cheers and petals and rice being thrown at them. Raúl's hand was hot on her waist, and he gripped her tighter when she nearly shot out of her dress at the sound of an explosion.

'It's firecrackers,' Raúl said. 'Sorry I forgot to warn you.'

And there would be firecrackers later too, Estelle thought, when they got to bed and she told him the truth! But it was far too late now to warn him.

It really was a wonderful wedding.

As Raúl had told her on the night they had met, there were no speeches; instead it was an endless feast, with dancing and celebration and congratulations from all.

She met Paola and Carlos, Raúl's aunt and uncle, and they spoke of Raúl's mother, Gabriella.

'She would be so proud to be here today,' Paola said. 'Wouldn't she, Antonio?'

Estelle saw how friendly they were with Raúl's father,

and also with Angela, who was naturally seated with them. No longer were they names, but faces, and a shiver went down her arms as she imagined their reaction when the truth came out.

'My son has excellent taste.' Antonio kissed her on the cheek.

Estelle had met him very briefly the day before, and Raúl had handled most of the questions—though both had seen the doubt in his eyes as to whether this union was real.

It was slowly fading.

'It is good to see my son looking so happy.'

He *did* look happy.

Raúl smiled at her as they danced their first dance as husband and wife, with the room watching on.

'Remember our first dance?' Raúl smiled.

'Well, we shan't be repeating *that* tonight.'

'Not till later.' Raúl gazed down, saw her burning cheeks, and mistook it for arousal.

He could never have guessed her fear.

'I ache to be inside you.'

Other couples had joined them. The music was low and sensual and it seemed to beat low in her stomach. His hand dusted her bare arm and she shivered at the thought of what was to come, wondered if those eyes, soft now with lust and affection, would darken in anger.

'Raúl…' Surely here was not the place to tell him, but it felt better with people around them rather than being alone. 'I'm nervous about tonight.'

'Why would you be nervous?' he asked. 'I will take good care of you.'

He would, Raúl decided. He was rarely excited at the thought of monogamy but he actually wanted to take care of her, could not stand to think of what she might have put her body through. There was a surge of protectiveness that shot through him then, and his arms tightened around her. He could feel her tension and nervousness and again he wanted to make her smile.

'Can I ask why,' he whispered into her ear as they danced, 'you embroidered a pineapple on my shirt?'

'It's a thistle!'

A smile spread on her lips and he felt her relax a little in his arms.

'For Scotland.'

Raúl found himself smiling too. 'All day I have been trying to work out the significance of a pineapple.'

She started to laugh and Raúl found himself laughing a little too.

He lowered his head and kissed her lightly.

It was expected, of course. What groom would *not* kiss his bride?

Many times since he had put his proposition to her Estelle had had doubts—the morality of it, the feasibility of it, the logistics—but as he kissed her, as she felt his warm lips and the soft caress of his hand near the base of her spine, true doubt as to her ability to go through with the deal surfaced. For once it had nothing to do with her hymen. She was suddenly more worried about her heart.

It was the music. It was the moment. It was having her brother here. It was Raúl's kiss. All these things, she told herself, were the reasons she felt as she did—as if this were real...as if this were love.

Estelle excused herself a little while later and went to the bathroom, just so she might collect herself, but brides could not easily hide on their wedding day.

'Estelle?' She turned at the sound of a woman's voice. 'I am Angela—Raúl's father's PA.'

'Raúl has spoken about you,' Estelle responded carefully.

'I'm sure what he had to say was not very flattering.' There were tears in the older woman's eyes. 'Estelle, I don't know what to believe…'

'Excuse me?'

'About this sudden marriage.' Angela was being as up-front with Estelle as she was with Raúl. 'I do know, though, that Raúl seems the happiest I have seen him. If you *do* love your husband…'

'If?'

'I apologise,' Angela said. 'Given that you surely love your husband, I ask this not for me, and not even for Antonio's sake. Whatever Raúl thinks of me, I care for him. I want him to come and visit us. I want us to be a family, even for a little while.'

'You could have had that years ago.' Estelle answered as she hoped Raúl would expect his loyal wife to.

'I want him to make peace with his father while there is still time. I don't want him to have any guilt when his father passes. I know how much guilt he has over his mother.'

Estelle blinked, unsure how to respond because there was so much she didn't know about Raúl. What did he have to feel guilty about? Raúl had been a child, after all. He had agreed to tell her more on their honeymoon—had said that he would be the one to deal with any questions tonight.

'I have always loved Raúl. I have always thought of him as a son.'

'So why did you leave it so late to tell him?' Perhaps it was the emotion of the day, but the tears that flashed in Estelle's eyes were real. 'If you cared so much for him—'

Estelle halted. It wasn't her place to ask, and Raúl certainly wouldn't thank her for delving. She was here to ensure his father left his share of the business to him, that was all. She would do well to remember that.

'I *do* care,' Angela responded. 'Whatever Raúl thinks of me, from a distance I have loved him as a son.'

'From a distance?' Estelle repeated, making the bitter point.

Turning on her heel, she walked out and straight into Raúl's arms.

'She wanted to speak about you,' Estelle told him. 'I don't know how well I handled it.'

'We'll discuss it later,' Raúl said, for he had seen Angela follow her in. 'Now we have to hand out the favours.'

It really was an amazing party, and for reasons of her own Estelle didn't particularly want it to end.

As per tradition, the bride and groom had to see off all their guests and be the last to leave. Antonio tired first, and she felt the grip of Raúl's hand tighten on hers as his father left with his loyal PA.

'It's been great,' Andrew said as he prepared to head back to the hotel he was staying in. 'Once Cecelia is well, and I'm working, I'm going to bring Amanda and Cecelia here for a holiday, to visit you.'

'You do that,' Estelle said, and bent down and gave her brother a cuddle, then stood as Raúl shook his hand.

'Look after my sister.'

'You do not have to worry about that.'

'Have a great honeymoon.'

A driver sorted out the wheelchair and they waved Andrew off and then headed back inside.

Apart from the staff it was just Raúl and Estelle now, and still the music went on as they danced their last dance of the night.

'It really helped having Andrew here.' Her hands were round the back of his neck, he held her hips, and she would give anything not to disappoint him tonight—anything to be the experienced lover he assumed she was.

'I thought it might.'

'It didn't just help me,' Estelle admitted, and started to tell him about how Andrew's confidence had been lacking.

But he dropped a kiss on her shoulder. 'Enough about others.'

Estelle swallowed. She could feel his fingers exploring the halter neck, his other hand running down the row of tiny buttons that ran to the base of her spine, and she knew he was planning his movements, undressing her slowly in his mind as they danced.

'Raúl...' His mouth was working over her bare shoulder, kissing it deeply; she could feel the soft suction, feel the heat of his tongue and his ardour building. 'I've never slept with anyone before.'

He moaned into her shoulder and pulled her tighter into him, so she could feel every inch of the turn-on he thought she was giving him.

'I mean it.' Her voice was shaking. 'You'll be my first.'

'Come on, then.' His mouth was now at her ear. 'Let's go and play virgins.'

CHAPTER TEN

THEY WERE DRIVEN the short distance to the marina, but for Estelle it just passed in a blur.

It was almost morning, yet despite the hour the celebrations continued.

Alberto, the skipper, welcomed them, and briefly introduced the staff—but Estelle barely took in the names, let alone her surroundings. All she could think of was what was soon to come as the crew toasted them and then Raúl dismissed them.

'Tomorrow I will show you around properly,' Raúl said, taking her champagne glass. 'But for now…'

There was no escaping. He pulled her towards him, his tongue back on her neck, at the crease between her neck and shoulder. He *had* been mentally undressing her before, for now his hands moved straight to the halter neck and expertly unravelled the carefully tied bow.

He had been expecting a basque, had anticipated another contraption to disable, but the dress had an inbuilt bra and he gave a low growl of approval as one of the breasts that had filled his private visions in recent days fell heavy and ripe into his palm.

'Raúl, someone might come…'

'That would be *you*,' he said, but she did not relax. 'No one will disturb us.'

Raúl lowered his head and licked around the pale areola, flicked a nipple that had been crushed all day by fabric back into rapid life, surprised that she was concerned that someone might come in. The staff on his yacht had seen many a decadent party—a husband and wife on their wedding night paled in comparison with what usually took place. He took the breast he craved in his mouth again, felt her hand try to push him back. He was at first surprised by her reticence—but then he remembered their game.

'Of course.' He smiled. 'You are nervous.'

He lifted her up and carried her down to the master stateroom, kissing her the entire way. He lowered her to the ground, turning her around so he could work on the tiny buttons from behind. It did not halt his mouth; his tongue kissed every inch of newly exposed flesh till her spine felt as if it were on fire.

He peeled off her dress, then her shoes and stockings. As his tongue licked and nibbled her sex through her silk panties the sensations his mouth delivered drove her wild. He only removed her panties when the moisture his mouth had made matched the dampening silk.

'Raúl…' Her hands were on his head—contrary hands that tried to halt him, while her moans of mounting desire urged him on.

'I want you so bad.' He peeled off her panties and, kneeling, parted her lips, his tongue darting to the swelling bud over and over as her hands knotted in his hair.

'Raúl…' she whimpered, lost between bliss and fear. 'I'm serious. I really haven't slept with anyone before.'

He simply didn't believe her. As she came under his mouth she had a hopeless thought that maybe he wouldn't guess, maybe he wouldn't know. Because despite her naïveté her body responded with ease. She throbbed against his mouth, more aroused than sated as he softly kissed the lingering orgasm.

He relished her taste, was assured she was moist. He was desperate now to take her.

He rose to his full height then, and shrugged his jacket off.

Breathless, aroused, moving on instinct, her hands shaking with want, she undid the buttons of his shirt. He was so dark and sultry, and he wore it well. His lips parted as her hands roamed his chest and she licked at his nipples as she undid his belt.

Raúl wanted her fingers at his zipper, and he wished she would hurry, but she lingered instead, feeling his thick heat through the fabric, her fingers lightly exploring. His already aching erection hardened further beneath her fingers. 'Estelle…' He could barely get the word out, but thankfully she read the urgency and slid the zipper down, and he let out a breath as she freed him.

He was delicious to her hands. She ran her fingers along his length, felt the soft skin that belied the strength beneath. She was petrified at the thought of him inside her, but wanting him just the same. She could see a trickle of silver and caught it with her finger, then swirled it around the head, entranced by its beauty.

Raúl closed his eyes in a mixture of frustration and bliss, for he wanted her hand to grip him tight, yet conversely he liked the tentative tease and exploration, liked the feel of her other hand gently weighing him.

Deeply they kissed, his tongue urging her to move faster, his erection twitching at the pleasure of her teasing, till he could take it no more.

'*Te quiero.*'

He told her he wanted her in Spanish as he pushed her

onto the bed. *'Tengo que usted tiene.'* He told her he had to have her as he parted her legs.

'Be gentle.' She was writhing and hot beneath him, her words contrary to the wanton woman in his arms. Her sex was slippery and warm and engorged as his hand stroked her there. She was as close to coming as Raúl, and his answer to her final plea was delivered as he nudged her entrance.

'It's way too late for gentle, baby.'

How he regretted those words as he seared and tore into her.

Raúl heard her sob, heard her bite back a scream.

Estelle knew then she had been a fool to think he might somehow not notice. He tore through her barrier but the pain did not end there. His fierce erection drove through tight muscles full of resistance. Too late to halt, too late to be tender, he froze—just not quickly enough. He leant on his elbows above her as she tried to work out how to breathe with Raúl inside her.

He attempted slow withdrawal. She begged that he did not. She lay there, trying to accommodate him, waiting for the heat and pain to subside, her muscles clamped around him.

'I take it out slowly,' Raúl said. He felt sick—appalled by his own brutality—and guilty too at the pleasure of her, hot and tight around him. He was so close to coming and trying to hold on. 'I'll just—'

'Don't.'

Her eyes were screwed tight as he moved a fraction backwards, but when he halted, when he stilled, her body relaxed a little. Estelle tried to release herself. She moved to slide away from him. Yet the pain was subsiding to a throbbing heat so she moved again, warming to the sensation of him inside her.

It was a different type of command she gave next. 'Don't stop.'

'Estelle?' He did not want to stop, and yet he did not want to hurt her; he moved slowly a little within her, his breath shallow, panting as if he had already come.

Her hands moved to his buttocks and she felt them tauten beneath her fingers. It was Estelle who pressed and dictated the tempo and, rarely for Raúl, he let her. Rarely for Raúl, he was humbled. He did not think of the questions he must ask her, just focused on the tight grip and the heat of her on his unsheathed skin, and all he could do was kiss her. Every inch of him held back, resisting the beckoning of oiled muscles that gripped as he slid past them, that urged him now to move faster, to take her deeper.

Estelle's breath was quickening. He felt the somewhat impatient rise of her groin, the press of her hands in his buttocks, and he could hold back no more.

Still he had not taken her fully, but now he thrust in. Estelle's neck arched as he probed and located fresh virgin flesh with each deepening thrust, and when he had filled her, when every part of her was consumed, he moved out and did it again, angling his hips, hitting her deep inside till she was moaning.

He was moving fast now, and she wrapped her legs around him, could not believe how her body had just taken over. For she lifted to him, was building to him, working with him, both heading to the same mutual goal.

No longer naïve, her body shattered in an orgasm like nothing she had ever given herself—for there she could stop, there she could halt. And it was nothing like the teasing he had given her either, for here in Raúl's bed he urged her on further, broke all limits, ensured that she screamed.

She pulsed around the head of him. He was stroking her deep inside—one spot that had her sobbing, one tender spot that he hit over and over—till she sobbed, and then he released himself into her. Her thighs were in spasm as a fresh wave of orgasm crashed through her body—and, yes, just as he had warned her, she cussed him in Spanish till he kissed her, till she was lying beneath him no longer a virgin.

She looked up at him, expecting a barrage of questions, a demand for an explanation, but instead he moved onto his side and put his arm around her, pulling her into him.

'I should have known' was his reprimand.

'I tried to tell you.'

'Estelle…' he warned.

She gave a small nod, conceding that tonight might have been rather too late.

'We will speak about it in the morning.'

For now, they held each other, lay in each other's arms, tired and sated and both in a place they had never thought they might be.

Estelle a bought bride; Raúl a man who had married and made love to a virgin.

CHAPTER ELEVEN

ESTELLE WOKE AND had no idea where she was for a moment.

Her body was bruised and sore. She could hear a shower.

She rolled over in bed and saw the evidence of their union, and moved the top sheet to cover it.

'Hiding the evidence?'

Estelle turned and was shocked at the sight of him. There was a towel round his hips, but his chest was covered in the bruises she now remembered her mouth making. He turned and took a drink from the breakfast table that had presumably been delivered and she saw the scratches on his back, remembered the wanton place he had taken her to.

'I need to have a shower.'

'We need to talk.' But then he conceded, 'Have some lunch and a shower. Then we will talk.'

'Lunch?'

'Late lunch,' Raúl said. 'It is nearly two.'

Estelle quickly gulped down some grapefruit juice and then headed to the bathroom. When she had found out they would be honeymooning on a yacht she had expected basic bathroom facilities; instead it was like a five-star hotel. The bathroom was marble, the taps and lighting incredible, yet she barely noticed. Her only thought was getting to her make-up bag.

The doctor had told her how important it was to take her pill on time every day. She was still getting used to it. Her breasts felt sore and tender, as if she were getting her period, and she still felt a little bit queasy from the new medication.

Estelle swallowed down the pill, making a mental note to change the alarm on her phone to two p.m.—or should she take it at seven tomorrow?

Her mind felt dizzy. She had seen that Raúl was less than impressed with her this morning and no doubt he would want a thorough explanation. She still hadn't worked out what to say.

Estelle showered and put on the factor fifty he insisted on, then sorted out her hair and make-up, relieved when she headed back into the bedroom and Raúl wasn't there. She selected a bikini from the many he had bought her, and also a pale lilac sarong. Her head was splitting from too much champagne and too much Raúl. She sat on the bed and put on espadrilles. Then, dressed—or rather barely dressed, as Raúl would want her to be—she stood. But her eyes did not go to the mirror—instead they went to the bed.

Mortified at the thought of a maid seeing the stained sheets, Estelle started to strip the bed.

'What are you doing?'

'I'm just making up the bed.'

'If I had a thing for maids then it would have been stipulated in the contract,' Raúl said. 'And if I had a thing for virgins,' he added, 'that would have been stipulated too.'

Estelle said nothing.

'Just leave it.' His voice was dark. 'The crew will take care of that. I will show you around.'

'I'll just wander…' She went to walk past.

'You can't hide from me here,' he warned, taking her wrist. 'But we will discuss it later. I don't want the staff getting even a hint that this is anything but a normal honeymoon.'

'Don't you trust your staff?' It was meant as a small dig—because surely a man in his position could easily pay for his privacy?

'I don't trust anyone,' Raúl said, watching the fire mount on her cheeks as his words sank in. 'And with good reason.'

She followed him up onto the deck. The sun blinded her for a moment.

'Where are your sunglasses?'

'I forgot to bring them.' She turned to head back down, but Raúl halted her, calling out to one of the crew. 'I can get them myself.'

'Why would you?'

Sometimes she forgot just how rich and spoilt he was. This was not one of those times. Despite the fact there were some of the crew around, he pulled her into his arms and very slowly kissed her.

'Raúl….' She was embarrassed by his passion. She looked into his black eyes and knew he was making a point.

'We are here for two days, darling. The plan is for us to fully enjoy them.'

His words were soft, the message not.

'I'll show you around now.'

A maid handed her her sunglasses and then Raúl showed her their abode for the next few days. The lounge that she had barely noticed last night was huge, littered with low sofas; another maid was plumping the cushions. There was a huge screen and, though nervous around him, Estelle did her best to be enthusiastic. 'This will be lovely for watching a movie.'

Raúl swallowed and caught the maid's eyes, and as Estelle went over to look at his DVD collection he quickly led her away.

'Here is the gym.' He opened a door and they stepped in. 'Not that you'll need it. I will ensure that you get plenty of exercise.'

Only there, with the door safely closed, did he let his true frustration slip out. He closed the door and gave her a glimpse of what was to come.

'If you think we are going to be sitting around watching movies and holding hands—'

'I know what I'm here for.'

'Make sure that you do.'

Raúl had woken at lunchtime from his first decent sleep in days, from his first night without nightmares. For a moment he had glimpsed peace—but then she had stirred in his arms and he had looked down to a curtain of raven hair and felt the weight of her breast on his chest. The sheet had tumbled from them; he'd seen her soft pale stomach and the evidence of their coupling on her inner thigh.

He had gone to move the sheet to cover them, but the movement had disturbed her a little and he had lain still, willing her back to sleep, fighting the urge to roll over and kiss her awake, make love to her again. He had felt the heat from her palm on his stomach and had physically ached for that hand to move down. His erection had been uncomfortable.

He'd fought the bliss of the memories of last night as his hand had moved down—and then halted when he'd realised his own thought-processes.

Sex Raúl could manage—and often.

Making love—no.

Last night had been but one concession, and he reminded himself she had lied.

He had removed her hand from him then and spent a

full ten minutes examining her face—from the freckles dusting her nose to the full lips that had deceived him.

He stood in the well-equipped gym and looked at them now. Absolutely he would make things clear.

'We have several weeks of this,' Raúl said. 'I wanted a woman who could handle my life, who knew how to have fun.' He did not mince words. 'Who was good in bed.'

He watched her cheeks burn.

'I'm sure I'll soon learn. I'll keep up my end of the deal—I don't need hand-holding.'

'There will be no holding hands.' He took her hand and placed it exactly where it had been agreed it would visit regularly. 'You knew what you were signing up for...'

He had to hold her back; he had to be at his poisonous worst. He could not simply dump her, as he usually did when a woman fell too hard. They had weeks of this and he could not risk her heart.

Instead he would put her to work.

'Let's have a spa.'

She saw the challenge in his eyes, knew that he was testing her, and smiled sweetly. 'Let's!'

She followed him up onto the deck, trying to ignore the fact that he had fully stripped off as she took off her espadrilles and dropped her sarong.

'Take off your top.'

'In a moment...'

He could sense rather than see that she was upset, and it made him furious. He was actually wishing his father dead, just so this might end.

'Take off your top,' he said again. Because if she thought she was here to discuss the passing scenery, or for them to get to know each other better, then she was about to find out she was wrong.

Estelle might have taken him for a fool.

He wasn't one.

Her face was one burning blush as her shaking hands undid the clasp, and she sank beneath the water as she removed it and placed the bikini top on the edge.

'Good morning!' The skipper made his way over. Naked breasts were commonplace on the Costa Del Sol—and especially on Raúl Sanchez Fuante's boat. He had no trouble at all looking Estelle in the eye as he greeted her. She, though, Raúl noted, was close to tears as she attempted to smile back.

'We are heading towards Acantilados de Maro-Cerro Gordo,' Alberto said, and then turned to Raúl. 'Would you like us to stop there tonight? The chef is looking forward to preparing your dinner and he wondered if you would like us to set up for you to eat on the bay?'

'We'll eat on the boat,' Raúl said. 'We might take a couple of jet skis out a little later and take a walk.'

'Of course,' Alberto said, then turned to Estelle.

'Do you have any preferences for dinner? Any food choices you would like the chef to know about?'

'Anything.'

Raul heard her try to squeeze the word out through breathless lips.

'It's a beautiful bay we are stopping at.' Albert happily chatted on. 'It's not far at all from the more built-up areas, but soon we will start to come into the most stunning virgin terrain.'

He wished them a pleasant afternoon and headed off.

'I've already explored the virgin terrain...' Raúl drawled, once he was out of earshot.

Estelle said nothing.

'Here.' Annoyed with himself for giving in, but hating her discomfort, he threw her the bikini top. 'Put it on if you want.'

She really was shaken, Raúl thought with a stab of guilt as he watched her trembling hands trying to put the damp garment on. Going topless was nothing here—nothing at all—but then he remembered last night: her shaking, her asking him to be gentle. Pleas he had ignored.

He strode through the water and turned her around, helping her with the clasp of her bikini top. Then, and he didn't know why, he pulled her into his arms and held her till she had stopped shaking—held her till the blush had seeped from her skin.

And then he made her burn again as he dropped a kiss on her shoulder and admitted a truth to her about that virgin terrain.

'...and it was stunning.'

CHAPTER TWELVE

NORMALLY RAÚL'S YACHT sailed into the busiest port, often with a party underway.

This early evening, though, they sailed slowly into Acantilados de Maro-Cerro Gordo. The sky was an amazing pink, the cliffs sparkling as they dropped anchor near a secluded bay.

'The beaches are stunning here,' Alberto said, 'and the tourists know it. But this one has no road access.' He turned to Raúl. 'The jet skis are ready for you both.'

Only as they were about to be launched did Raúl remember. He turned and saw her pale face, saw that she was biting on her lip as she went to climb on the machine, and his apology was genuine.

'Estelle, I'm sorry. I forgot about your brother's accident.'

'It's fine,' she said through chattering teeth. 'He was showing off…mucking around…' She was trying to pretend that the machine she was about to climb on *didn't* petrify her. 'I know we'll be sensible.'

Raúl had had no intention of being sensible. He loved the exhilaration of being on a jet ski and had wanted to share it with her—had wanted to race and to chase.

Instead he was taking her hand. 'It's not fine. You don't have to pretend.'

Oh, but she did. At every turn she had to pretend, if she was to be the temporary woman he wanted.

'Come on this one with me,' Raúl said. 'Alberto, take her hand and help her on.'

They rode towards the bay in a rather more subdued fashion than Raúl was used to.

The maid who was setting up the dinner table caught Alberto's eye when he came to check on her progress and they shared a brief smile.

His bride and the effect she was having on Raúl was certainly not one they had been expecting.

'I think I might go and reorganise his DVD collection,' the maid suggested and Alberto nodded.

'I think that might be wise.'

Estelle held tightly onto Raul's waist as the jet ski chopped through the waves, and because her head kept knocking into his back in the end she gave in and rested it there, not sure if her rapid heart-rate was because she was scared by the vehicle, by the questions she would no doubt soon be facing, or just by the exhilaration.

Making love with Raúl had been amazing. She was sore and tender but now, feeling his skin beneath her cheek, feeling the ocean water sting her and the wind whip her hair, she could not regret a moment. Even her lie. Feeling his passion as he had seared into her was a memory she would be frequently revisiting. For now, though, Estelle knew she had to play it tough—had to convince him better than she had so far that she was up to the job he had paid her for.

He skidded into the shallows and she unpeeled herself from him and stepped down.

'It's amazing…' She looked up at the cliffs, shielding her eyes. 'Look how high it is.'

He did, but only briefly. Estelle was too busy admiring the stunning view to notice his pallor.

'What did Angela say to you at the wedding?' Raúl asked.

She had been expecting a barrage of questions about her lack of experience, and was momentarily sideswiped at his choice of topic for conversation, but then she reminded herself his interest in her was limited.

'She wasn't sure whether or not we were a true couple,' Estelle said.

'You corrected her?'

'Of course,' Estelle said. 'She seems to think that *if* I love my husband, then I should encourage you to make peace with your father while there is still time.' She glanced over to him as they walked. 'She wants us to go there and visit.'

'It is too late to play happy families.'

'Angela said that she doesn't want you to suffer any guilt, as you did over your mother's death…'

'Misplaced guilt,' Raúl said, but didn't elaborate any more.

He stopped and they sat on the beach, looking out to the yacht. She could see the lights were on, the staff on deck were preparing their meal. It was hard to believe such luxury even existed, let alone that for now it was hers to experience. It was the luxury of *him* she wanted, though; there was more about Raúl that she needed to know.

'I didn't know how to answer her,' Estelle admitted. 'You said there was more you would tell me. I have no real idea about your family, nor about you.'

'So I will tell you what you need to know.' He pondered for a moment on how best to explain it. 'My grandfather—my mother's father—ran a small hotel. It did well and he built another, and then he purchased some land in the north,' Raúl explained.

'In San Sebastian?' Estelle asked.

He nodded. 'On his death the business was left to his three children—De La Fuente Holdings. My father and mother married, and my father started to work in the family business. But he was always an outsider—or felt that he was, even though he oversaw the building of the San Sebastian hotel. When I was born my mother became unwell. In hindsight I would say she was depressed. It was then he started to sleep with Angela. Apparently Angela felt too much guilt and left work, moved back to her family, but they started seeing each other again...'

'How do you know all this?'

'My father told me the morning I met you.'

It was only then that Estelle fully realised this was almost as new to him as it was to her.

'Angela got pregnant, the guilt ate away at him, and he told my mother the truth. He wanted to know if she could forgive him. She cried and wailed and screamed. She told him to get out and he went to Angela—the baby was almost due. He assumed my mother would tell her family, that she would turn to them. Except she did not. When she had the car accident and died my father returned and soon realised no one knew he had another son. Instead they welcomed him back into the company.' He was silent for a moment. 'Soon they will find out the truth.'

'Angela said that you blamed yourself for your mother's death?'

'That is all you need to know.' He looked over to her. 'Your turn.'

'I don't know what to tell you.'

'Why you lied?'

'I didn't lie.'

'The same way my father didn't lie when he didn't tell me had another son? The same way Angela didn't lie when she failed to tell mention her son, Luka, was my brother?' He did not want to think about that. 'Okay, if you didn't outright lie, you *did* deceive.'

He watched her swallow, watched as her face jerked away to look out to the ocean.

'I wanted an experienced woman.'

'Sorry I don't know enough tricks—'

'I wasn't talking about *sex*!' Raúl hurled. 'I wanted a woman who could handle things. Who could keep to a deal. Who wasn't going to fall in love…'

'Again you assume!' Estelle flared. 'Why would I fall in love with some cold bastard who thinks only in money—who has no desire for true affection? A man who tells me what to wear and whether or not I can tan.'

Her eyes flashed as she let out some of the anger she had suppressed over the past few days while every decision apart from her wedding dress had been made by him.

'Raúl, I would not have a man choose my clothes or dictate to the hairdresser the style of my hair, or the beautician the colour of my nails. You're getting what you paid for—what you wanted—what you demanded. Consider my virginity a bonus!'

She dug her heels deep into the sand and almost believed her own words. Tried to ignore that last night, as she'd been falling asleep in his arms, foolish thoughts had invaded. Raúl's doubts about her ability to see this through perhaps had merit, for he would be terribly easy to love…

She turned around and faced him.

'I'm here for the money, Raúl.' And not for a single second more would she allow herself to forget it. 'I'm here with you for the same reason I was with Gordon.'

He could not stand the thought of her in bed with him—

could not bear to think about it. But when he did, Raúl frowned.

'If you were with Gordon for money, how come you were trying to change the sheets before the maid got in.'

'I was never with Gordon in that way. I just stood in for Ginny.'

'You shared his bed,' Raúl said. 'And we all know his reputation…'

'Unlike you, Gordon didn't feel comfortable going to a wedding alone,' Estelle said carefully.

'So he paid you to look like his tart?' Raúl checked. 'What about Dario's…?' His voice trailed off and he frowned as he realised the lengths Gordon had gone to, then frowned a little more as realisation hit. 'Is Gordon…?' He didn't finish the question—knew it was none of his business. 'You needed the money to help out your brother?'

She conceded with a nod.

'Estelle, it is not for me to question your reasons—'

'Then don't.'

Her warning did not stop him.

'Andrew would not want it.'

'Which is why he will never find out.'

'I know that if I had a sister I would not want her—'

'Don't compare yourself to my brother. You don't even have a sister, and the brother you *do* have you don't want to know.'

'What's that got to do with it?'

'We're two very different people, Raúl. If I discovered that I had a brother or sister somewhere I'd be doing everything I could to find out about them, to meet them—not plotting to bring them down.'

'I'm not plotting anything. I just don't want him taking what is rightfully mine. Neither do I want to end up working alongside him.'

She looked at the seductive eyes that invited you only to bed, at the mouth that kissed so easily but insisted you did not get close.

'You miss out on so much, Raúl.'

'I miss out on nothing,' Raúl said. 'I have everything I want.'

'You have everything money can buy,' Estelle said, remembering the reason she was here. 'Including me.'

When he kissed her it tasted of nothing. It tasted empty. It was a pale comparison to the kiss he had been the recipient of last night. And when he took her top off he knew she was faking it, knew she was thinking of the boat and of people watching, knew she was trying not to cry.

'Not here,' Raúl said for her.

'Please, Raúl...'

Her mouth sought his. She was still playing the part, too inexperienced to understand that he knew her body lied.

He wanted it back, the intimacy of last night, which meant taking care of her.

For now.

Surely for a couple of days he could take care of her. They could just enjoy each other and break her in properly. The last thing he wanted was her tense and teary, feeling exposed.

He had glimpsed her toughness, admired the lengths she would go to for her family, and he believed her now—she did not want his love

'Later.' Raúl pulled his head back from her mouth. 'I'm starving.'

He helped her with her bikini, used his chest as a shield as he did up the clasp, just in case any passing fish were having a peek, or telescopes were trained on them. But rather than making him feel irritated, her coyness now made him smile.

Especially when he thought of her unleashed.

'Come on,' Raúl said, despite the ache in his groin. 'Let's head back.'

CHAPTER THIRTEEN

'WE WILL GO and shower and get dressed for dinner,' Raúl said as they boarded and Alberto took the jet ski. 'Do you want me to ask Rita to come down and do your hair?'

'Rita?'

'She is a masseuse and a beautician. If you want her to come and help just ask Alberto,' Raúl said, heading off to the stateroom.

Estelle called him back. She could smell the food and was honestly starving. 'Why do we have to get dressed for dinner?' Estelle did not notice the twitch of his lips, though Alberto did. 'It's only us.'

'On a yacht such as this one, when the chef...' Raúl began. But he was torn, because etiquette often had no place on board and it seemed petty to put her right. 'Very well.' He turned to Alberto, who was already on to it.

'I'll let the chef know.'

They rinsed off under the shower on deck and then took their seats.

Raúl was rather more used to a well-made-up blonde in a revealing dress sitting opposite him, but there was something incredibly appealing about sitting for dinner half-naked and scooping up the delicacies the waiters were bringing.

'I could get far too used to this,' Estelle started, and

then stopped herself, remembering his words at the lawyer's. 'I meant…'

'I know what you meant.'

She was relieved to see he was smiling.

'The food really is amazing,' Raúl agreed. 'They chef is marvellous. Chefs on yachts generally are—that is why we keep coming back for more.'

They chatted as they ate, far more naturally than they had before, and it wasn't just for the benefit of the staff.

It was simply a blissful night.

They danced.

On the deck of his yacht they danced when the music came on.

'I understand now why we should have changed for dinner,' Estelle admitted. 'Do you think I've offended anyone?'

'I don't think you could if you tried.'

The sky was darkening and Raúl looked out to the cliffs, and rather than remembering hell he buried his face in her hair. It took only the smell of the ocean in her hair for him to escape.

'And for the record,' Raúl said, 'although you accuse me being a controlling bastard, I was worried about you burning. I have never seen paler skin.'

'I think I *am* a bit sunburnt.'

'I know.'

They moved down to the lounge room. Estelle was starting to relax—so much so that she didn't spring from his arms when some dessert wine was brought through to them.

'Let's go to bed…' His hand was in her bikini top, trying to free her breast.

'Not yet,' she breathed into his mouth. 'I'll never sleep.'

'I have no intention of letting you sleep.'

'Let's watch a movie,' Estelle said, unwrapping herself from him and heading over to his collection.

'Estelle—no!'

'Oh, sorry.' She'd forgotten what he'd told her in the gym, about no hand-holding and movies, and she turned and attempted a smile. 'Sure—let's go to bed.'

'I didn't mean that,' Raúl said through gritted teeth, wondering how he'd ended up with the one hooker to whom he'd have to apologise for his DVDs. 'I just don't think there will be anything there to your taste.'

He braced himself for the rapid demise of a pleasant night as Estelle flicked through his collection.

'I love this one.'

'Really?' Raúl was very pleasantly surprised.

'Actually…' She skimmed through a couple more. 'This one's my favourite.' She held up the cover to him and didn't understand his smile.

'Of course it is,' Raúl said, pulling her down beside him, smiling into her hair. One day he would tell her how funny that was—one day when it wouldn't offend, when she knew him better. He would laugh about it with her.

But there would not *be* that day, he reminded himself. This was just for now.

He had not lain on a sofa and watched a movie—not one with a plot, anyway—since he couldn't remember when.

Estelle shivered. The doors were open and the air was cooling. He pulled down a rug from the back of the sofa and covered them, felt her bottom curving into him.

'Sore?' He kissed her pink shoulders as he made light work of her bikini top.

'A bit.'

Estelle concentrated on the movie as Raúl concentrated on Estelle. He kissed her neck and shoulders for ages, then played with her breasts, massaging them with his palms, taking her nipples between thumb and fingers. Then slowly, when he knew there would be no qualms from Estelle, moved one hand down and untied her bikini bottoms.

His question, when repeated, was a far more personal one as his fingers crept in.

'Sore?'

'A bit,' she said again, but he was so gentle, and it felt so sublime.

She could feel the motion of the boat, and him huge and hard behind her; she could feel the urging of his mouth to turn to him and growing insistence from behind.

'Turn around, Estelle.' His breathing was ragged.

'In a minute.' She wasn't even watching the film. Her eyes were closed. She was just loving the feel of him playing with her and longing for it to go on. 'It's coming to the best bit.'

He pulled her up a little further, so that her naked bum was against his stomach, and he angled her perfectly. She felt the long, slow slide of him where he had stabbed into her last night. She was still bruised and swollen and hot down below, and yet she closed around him in relief.

'*This* is the best bit,' Raúl's low voice corrected her.

He pressed slowly into her, his fingers playing with her clitoris, slid slowly and deeply, with none of the haste of last night, and it was Estelle who was fighting to hold back.

'I'm going to come.'

'Not yet,' he told her, teasing her harder with his fingers, thrusting himself deeper inside.

'I am.' She was trembling and trying to hold on.

'Not yet.'

He stroked her somewhere so deep, the feeling so intense that she let out a small squeal.

'There?' he asked.

Estelle didn't know what he meant, but then he stroked her there again and she sobbed. 'There!' She was begging as over and over he massaged her deep, hitting her somewhere she hadn't even known existed. 'There…'

She was starting to cry, but with intense pleasure, and then she could no longer hold it. There was no point even trying.

There was a flood of release as she pulsed around him, and Raúl moaned as she tightened over and over around his thick length. He felt the rush of her orgasm flowing into him and he shot back in instant response, spilling deep into her, loving her abandon, loving the Estelle his body revealed.

Loving too the tinge of embarrassment that crept in as she struggled to get her breath back.

'What was that?'

'Us,' he said, still inside her. And it was not the cliffs he feared now, but the perfume of the ocean in her hair as he inhaled it—a fear that was almost overwhelming as he realised how much he had enjoyed this night.

Not just the sex, not just the talking, not just dinner.

But *now*.

'We should head back.'

They had been snorkelling. It had all started off innocently, but had turned into a slightly more grown-up activity. Raúl did not know if it was her laughter, or the feel of her legs wrapped around him, or just that he was simply enjoying her too much, but he kissed her cheek and unwrapped her legs from his waist.

'Is it dinner-time?'

'I meant we should head back for Marbella…'

It had been two nights and two amazing days, and more of a honeymoon than Raúl had ever intended for it to be.

They *were* dressing for dinner tonight, because they wouldn't be dawdling on their return. Which meant this would be their last night on the yacht.

She missed it already.

Even as Rita did her hair and make-up she missed the yacht, because it had been the most magical time. As if they had suspended the rules of the contract, their time had been spent talking, laughing, eating, making love—but Raúl had made it clear that things would be different when they returned to Marbella.

She felt as if they were approaching that already as Rita pushed the last pin into Estelle's hair. Raúl's expression was tense as he picked up his ringing phone.

'I will tell the chef you will be up soon,' Rita said, and Estelle thanked her and started to put on her dress.

She didn't understand what was being said on the phone, but given the terse words, she guessed it wasn't pleasant.

'They are getting married.' Raúl hung up and was silent.

By the time he told her what the call had been about he was doing up his tie, but kept getting the knot wrong.

'Oh.' She didn't know what else to say, just went on struggling with her zip.

'Come here.' He found the side zipper. 'It's stuck.'

She stood still as he tried to undo it.

'My father says he wants to do the right thing by Angela—wants to give her the dignity of being his wife and his widow. He wants her to have a say in decisions by the medical staff.'

'What did you say?'

'That it was the first decent thing I had heard on the subject.'

'Are you going to attend?'

He didn't answer her question; instead he hurried her

along. 'Come on. They will be serving up soon. It is not fair to keep the chef waiting.'

Since when was Raúl thoughtful about his staff? Estelle thought, but said nothing.

It was an amazing dinner. The chef had made his own paella, and even Raúl agreed, it was the best he had tasted.

Yet he barely touched it.

He looked at Estelle; she looked exquisite. Her hair was up, as it had been on their wedding day, her black dress looked stunning, and he told himself he could do it—that it wasn't a problem after all.

'What would you think if we did not turn around for Marbella?'

Estelle swallowed the food she was relishing and took a drink of water, nervous for the same reasons as Raúl.

'We could head to the islands, extend our trip…'

'So that you miss your father's wedding?'

'He has chosen to marry when I am on my honeymoon. He doesn't know we were to be on our way back.'

'You'll have to face him at some point.'

'You don't tell me what I have to do!' he snapped, and then righted himself, trying to explain things a little better. 'He wants a wedding—one happy memory with his wife. I doubt that will be manageable with me there. Especially if Luka attends.' He took a breath. 'So how about a few more days?' He made it sound so simple. 'I have not had a proper holiday in years…'

'I thought your life was one big holiday?'

'No,' Raúl said. 'My life is one big party. We will return to that in a few days.' He issued it as a warning, telling her without saying as much that what happened at sea stayed at sea.

He was waiting for her decision. But then Raúl remembered the decision was entirely his. He was paying for her company—not her say in their location.

'I will let the staff know.'

'Now?'

'They have to plot the route, inform…'

He didn't finish, just headed off to let the crew know, and Estelle sat there, suddenly nervous.

She wanted to be back on safe water—because living with Raúl like this, seeing this side of him, she was struggling to remember the rules.

Their 'couple of days' turned into two weeks.

They sailed around Menorca and took their time exploring its many bays. Estelle's skin turned from pale to pink, from freckles to brown. He watched her get bolder, loved seeing her stretch out on a lounger wearing only bikini bottoms, not even a little embarrassed now. Her sexuality was blossoming to his touch, before his eyes.

Finally they sailed back into Marbella. Normally the sight of it was the one he loved best in the world, yet there was a moment when he wanted to tell the skipper to keep sailing, to bypass Marbella and head to Gibraltar, take the yacht to Morocco, just to prolong their time. Except he was growing far too fond of her.

She put a hand on his shoulder, joined him to watch the splendid sight, but she felt his shoulder tense beneath her touch.

Raúl turned. She was wearing espadrilles and bikini bottoms, his own wedding shirt knotted beneath her now rosy bust, her cheeks flushed and her lips still swollen from their recent lovemaking.

'You'd better get dressed.'

Usually Raúl was telling her she was *over*dressed.

'The press may be there. The cream dress,' he told her. 'And have Rita do your make-up.'

As easily at that he demoted her, reminded her of her place.

Back on dry land he took her hand. But it was just for the cameras that he put his shoulders around his new wife.

It was in case of a long lens that he picked up her and carried her into his apartment, back to the reality of his life.

CHAPTER FOURTEEN

IT WAS A life she could never have imagined.

Raúl worked harder than anyone she knew.

His punishing day started at six, but rather than coming in drained at the end of it he would have a quick swim in the pool, or they'd make love—or rather they'd have sex. Because the Raúl from the yacht was gone now. A quick shower after that and then they'd get changed for dinner. Meals were always eaten out, and then they would hit the pulsing nightlife, dancing and partying into the early hours.

Estelle couldn't believe this was the toned-down version of Raúl.

'I can cook,' Estelle said, and smiled one night as they sat at Sol's and waited for their dishes to be served. 'It might be a novelty…'

'Why would you cook when a few steps away you can have whatever you choose?'

It was how he lived: life was a smorgasbord of pleasure. But six weeks married to Raúl, even with a week off to visit her family, was proving exhausting for Estelle—and she wasn't the one working. Or rather, she corrected herself as the waiter brought her a drink, she *was* working, twenty-four-seven, because no way would she be dining out every night, no way would she be wandering along streets that still pumped with music well after midnight on a Tuesday.

It had been Cecelia's cardiology appointment today, and Estelle was worried sick and doing her best not to show it. But she kept glancing at her phone, willing it to ring, wondering when she'd hear.

'How's your new PA?' Estelle asked as she bit into the most gorgeous braised beef, which had been cooked over an open fire.

'Okay.' Raúl shrugged. 'Angela trained her well...'

He looked down at her plate, stabbed a piece of beef with a fork and helped himself. Estelle was getting used to the way they shared their meals; it was the norm here.

'It *is* much more difficult without Angela,' Raúl admitted. 'Only now she is gone are we seeing how much she did around the place.'

'When will she be back?'

'She won't,' Raúl said. 'She is taking long service leave to nurse my father. Once he dies and it gets out about her she won't be welcome there.'

'Oh, well, you'll only have to see her at the funeral, then.'

Raúl glanced up. He could never be sure if she was being flip or serious. 'When are you going to see your father?' she asked him.

She was being serious, Raúl quickly found out.

'He chose to live in the north—he chose to end his days with his other family. Why should I....?' He closed his tense lips. 'I do not want to discuss it.'

'Angela called again today.'

'I told you not answer to her.'

'I was waiting for my brother to ring,' Estelle said. 'It was Cecelia's cardiology appointment today. I didn't think to look when I picked up.' Estelle could not finish her dinner and pushed the plate away.

'You're not hungry?'

'Just full.'

'I was thinking…' Raúl said. 'There is a show premiering in Barcelona at the weekend. I think it might be something we would enjoy.'

'Raúl…' She just could not sit and say nothing—could not lie beside him at night and sleep with him without caring even a bit, without having an opinion. Surely he could understand that? 'I was riddled with guilt when my parents died.'

'Why?'

'For every row, for every argument—for all the things we beat ourselves up about when someone dies. Guilt happens whatever you do. Why not make it about something you couldn't have changed, instead of something you can?' On instinct she went to take his hand, but he pulled it back.

'You're starting to sound like a wife.'

She looked at him.

'Believe me, I don't feel like one.'

Estelle pounced on her phone when it rang.

'I need to take this.'

'Of course.'

It was Amanda, doing her best, as always, to sound upbeat. 'They're going to keep Cecelia in for a few nights. She's a bit dehydrated…'

'Any idea when she's going to have surgery?'

'She's too small,' Amanda said. 'They've put a tube in, and we're going to be feeding her through that. She might come home on oxygen…'

Raúl watched Estelle's eyes filling with tears but she turned her shoulders and hunched into the phone in an effort to hide them. He heard her attempt to be positive even while she was twisting her hair around and around her finger.

'She's a fighter,' Estelle said, but as she did so she closed her eyes.

'How is your niece?' Raúl asked as she rang off.

'Much the same.' She didn't want to discuss it for fear she might break down—Raúl would be horrified! Seeing that he'd finished eating, Estelle gave him a bright smile. 'Where do you want to go next?'

'Where do *you* want to go?' Raúl offered.

Home, her body begged as they walked along the crowded street. But that wasn't what she was here for. She'd been transferring money over to Andrew since he'd gone back to England. The first time she'd told Andrew it was money she'd been saving to get a car. The second time she'd said it was a loan. Now she'd just given him a decent sum that would see them through the next few months, telling Andrew that she and Raúl simply wanted to help.

It was time to earn her keep.

They passed a club that was incredibly loud and very difficult to get into. It was a particular favourite of Raúl's. 'How about here?'

Estelle woke to silence. It was ten past ten and Raúl would long since have gone to work.

She sat up in bed and then, feeling dizzy, lay back down.

How the hell he lived like this on a permanent basis, Estelle had no idea. All she knew was she was not going out tonight.

He could, she decided, dressing and heading out not for the trendy boutiques but for the markets. She just wanted a night at home—or rather a night in Raúl's home—and something simple for dinner. There must be some subclause in the contract that allowed for the occasional night off?

Marbella was rarely humid, the mountains usually shielded it, but it struggled today. The air was thick and oppressive and the markets were very busy. Estelle had bought the ripest, plumpest vine tomatoes, and was deciding between lamb and steak when she passed a fish stall and gave a small retch. She tried to carry on, to continue walking, tried to focus on a flower stall ahead instead of the appalling thought she had just had.

She couldn't be pregnant.

Estelle took her pill at the same time every day.

Or she had tried to.

All too often Raúl would come home at lunchtime, or they'd be in a helicopter flying anywhere rather than to his father's—the one place he needed to be.

She couldn't be pregnant.

'Watch where you're going!' someone scolded in Spanish as she bumped into them.

'Lo sierto,' Estelle said, changing direction and heading for the *Pfarmacia*, doing the maths in her head and praying she was wrong.

Less that half an hour later she found out she was right.

Raúl didn't get home from work till seven, and when he did it was to the scent of bread baking and the sight of Estelle in his underutilised kitchen, actually cooking.

'Are we taking the wife thing a bit far?' Raúl checked tentatively. 'You don't have to cook.'

'I want to,' Estelle said. She was chopping up a salad. 'I just want to have a night in, Raúl.'

'Why?'

'Because.' She frowned at him. 'Do you ever stop?'

'No,' he admitted, then came over and give her a kiss. 'Are you okay?'

'I'm fine. Why?'

'You didn't wake up when I left this morning. You seem tense.'

'I'm worried about my niece,' Estelle said, removing herself from him and adding two steaks to the grill.

She was curiously numb. Since she'd done the test Estelle had been operating on autopilot and baking bread, which she sometimes did when she didn't want to think.

She just couldn't play the part tonight.

They carried their food out to the balcony and ate steak and tomato salad, with the herb bread she had made, watching a dark storm rolling in.

Estelle wanted to go home, wanted this over. Though she knew there was no getting out of their deal. But she needed a timeframe more than ever now. She wanted to be far away from him before the pregnancy started showing.

She could never tell him.

Not face to face, anyway.

Estelle could not bear to watch his face twist, to hear the accusations he would hurl, for him to find another reason not to trust.

'I spoke with my father today.'

She tore her eyes from the storm to Raúl. 'How is he?'

'Not good,' Raúl said. 'He asks that I go and see him soon.'

'Surely you can manage to be civil for a couple of days?' She was through worrying about saying the wrong thing. 'Yes, your father had an affair, but clearly it meant something. They're together all this time later...'

'An affair that led to my mother's death.' He stabbed at his steak. 'Their lies left the guilt with *me*.' He pushed his plate away.

The eyes that lifted to hers swirled with grief and confusion and now, when all she wanted was to be away from him, when she must guard her heart properly, when she needed it least, Raúl confided in her.

'I had an argument with my mother the night she died. She had missed my performance at the Christmas play—as she missed many things. When I came home she was crying and she said sorry. My response? *Te odio.* I told her I hated her. That night she lifted me from my sleep and put me in a car. The mountains are a different place in a storm,' Raúl explained. 'I had no idea what was happening; I thought I had upset her by shouting. I told her I was sorry. I told her to slow down...'

Estelle could not imagine the terror.

'The car skidded and came off the mountain, went down the cliffside. My father returned from his so-called work trip to be told his wife was dead and his son was in hospital. He chose not to tell anyone the reason he'd been gone.'

'Did they never suspect he and Angela?'

'Not for a moment. He just seemed to be devoting more and more time to the hotel in San Sebastian. Angela was from the north and she resumed working for him again. Over the years, clearly when Luka was older, she started to come to Marbella more often with my father. We had a flat for her, which she stayed in during the working week.'

'He had two sons to support,' Estelle said. 'Maybe it was the only way he could see how.'

'Please!' Raúl scoffed. 'He was with Angela every chance he could get, leaving me with my aunt and uncle. Had he wanted one family he could have had it. Perhaps it would have been a struggle, but his family would have been together. He chose this life, and those choices caused my mother's death.'

'Instead of you?'

'I blamed myself for years for her death. I thought the terrible things I said…'

'You were a child.'

'Yes,' he said. 'I see that now. The night she died was two days after Luka's birth. I realise now that she was on her way to confront them.'

'In a storm, with a five-year-old in the back of her car,' Estelle pointed out.

'I thought she was trying to kill me.'

'She was ill, Raúl.'

He nodded. 'It would have been nice to know that she was,' Raúl said. 'It would have been nice to know that it was not my words that had her fleeing into the night.'

'It sounds as though she was sick for a long time, and I would imagine it was a very tough time for your father…' Estelle did not want involvement. She wanted to remove herself as much as she could before she told him. Yet she could not sit back and watch his pain. 'He just wants to know you're happy, that you're settled. He just wants peace.'

'We all want peace.' He was a moment away from telling her the rest, but instead he stood and headed through the balcony door. 'I'm going out.'

Estelle sat still.

'Don't wait up.'

'I won't.'

She didn't want him going out in this mood, and she followed him into the lounge while knowing he wouldn't welcome her advice. 'Raúl, I don't think—'

'I don't pay you to think.'

'You're upset.'

'Now she tells me what I'm *feeling*!'

'Now *she* reminds you that she read that contract before she signed it. If you think you're going to go out clubbing and carrying on in your usual way I'll be on the next plane home…' she watched his shoulders stiffen '…with every last cent you agreed to pay me.'

He headed for the door.

'Hope the music's loud enough for you, Raúl!' she called out to him.

'It could never be loud enough.'

There was a crack from the storm and the balcony doors flew wide open. He turned then, and she glimpsed hell in his eyes. There was more than he was telling her, she knew that, and yet she did not need to know at this moment.

He was striding towards her and she understood for a moment his need for constant distraction, for *she* was craving distraction now. She was pregnant by the man she loved, who was incapable of loving her. How badly she didn't want to think about it. How nice it would be for a moment to forget.

His mouth was, perhaps for the last time, welcome. The crush of his lips was so fierce he might have drawn blood. Yet it was still not enough. He wrestled her to the floor and it was still too slow.

Here beneath him there were no problems—just the weight of him on her.

He was pulling at his zipper and pressing up her skirt. She was kissing him as if his lips could save them both. The balcony doors were still wide open. It was raining on the inside, raining on them, yet it did not douse them.

He had taught her so much about her body, but she learned something new now—how fast her arousal could be.

He was coming even before he was inside her; she could feel the hot splash on her sex. Estelle was sobbing as he thrust inside her, holding onto him for dear life. Each thrust of his hips met with her own desperation. It was fast and it was brutal, and yet it was the closest they had ever been.

He was at her ear and breathing hard when he lifted his face. She opened her eyes to a different man.

'Come with me to see them?'

He was asking, not telling.

'Yes.'

'Tomorrow?'

'Yes.'

It felt terribly close to love.

CHAPTER FIFTEEN

THEY FLEW EARLY the next morning, over the lush hills of Spain to the north, and even as his jet made light work of the miles there was a mounting tension. Had they run out of time?

Far from anger from Raúl, there was relief when Angela came out of the door to greet them, a wary smile on her face.

'Come in,' she said. 'Welcome.'

She gave Estelle a kiss on the cheek, and gave one too to Raúl. 'We can do this,' she said to him, even as he pulled back. 'For your father. For one day…'

Raúl nodded and they headed through to the lounge.

If Estelle was shocked at the change in his father, it must be hell for Raúl.

'Hey,' he greeted his son. 'You took your time.'

'I'm here now,' Raúl said. 'Congratulations on your wedding.' He handed Antonio a bottle of champagne as he kissed him on the cheek. 'I thought we could have a toast to you both later.'

'I finally make an honest woman of her,' Antonio said.

Estelle watched as Raúl bit back a smart response. There really was no time for barbs.

'Your brother is flying in from Bilbao tonight. Will you stay for dinner?' Antonio's eyes held a challenge.

'I'm not sure that we can stay…'

'A meeting between the two of you is inevitable,' Antonio said. 'Unless you boycott my funeral. I am to be buried here,' he added.

She watched Raúl's jaw tighten as he told his son that this was the home he loved. Yet he had denied his first son the chance of having a real home.

'I will make a drink,' Angela said to Estelle. 'Perhaps you could help me?'

Estelle went into the kitchen with her. It was large and homely, and even though she was hoping to keep things calm for Raúl, Estelle was angry on his behalf.

'We will leave them to it,' Angela said as Estelle sat at the table. 'You look tired.'

'Raúl doesn't live a very quiet life.'

'I know.' Angela smiled and handed her a cup of hot chocolate and a plate of croissants.

Estelle took a sip of her chocolate, but it was far too sickly and she put the cup back down.

'I can make you honey tea,' Angela offered. 'That is what I had when…' Her voice trailed off as she saw the panic in Estelle's eyes and realised she must not want anyone to know yet. To Angela it was obvious—she hadn't seen Estelle since her wedding day, and despite the suntan her face was pale, and there were subtle changes that only a woman might notice. 'Perhaps your stomach is upset from flying.'

'I'm fine,' Estelle said, deliberately taking another sip.

'I am worried that when Antonio dies I will see no more of Raúl…'

Estelle bit her lip. Frankly she wouldn't blame him. Because being here, seeing first-hand evidence of years of lies and deceit, she understood a little better the darkness of his pain.

'He is like a son to me.'

Estelle simply couldn't stay quiet. 'From a distance?' She repeated Angela's own words from the wedding day and then looked around. There were pictures of Luka, who looked like a younger Raúl.

'Raúl is here too.' Angela pointed to a photo.

'He wasn't, though.' Estelle could not stand the pretence. 'You had a home here—whereas Raúl was being shuffled between his aunt and uncle, occasionally seeing his dad.'

'It was more complicated than that.'

'Not really.' Estelle simply could not see it. 'You say you think of him as a son, and yet…'

'We did everything the doctor said,' Angela wrung her hands. 'I need to tell you this—because if Raúl refuses to speak with me ever again, then this much I would like you to know. The first two years of Luka's life Antonio hardly saw him. He did everything to help Raúl get well, and that included keeping Luka a secret. The doctor said Raul needed his home, needed familiarity. How could we rip him away from his family and his house? How could we move him to a new town when the doctor insisted on keeping things as close to normal as possible?'

Estelle gave a small shrug. 'It would have been hard on him, but surely no harder than losing his mother. He thought it was because of something he had said to her.'

'How could we have known that?'

'You could have spoken to him. You could have asked him about what happened. Instead you were up here, with his dad.'

There was a long stretch of silence, finally broken by Angela. 'Raúl hasn't told you, has he?'

'He's told me everything.'

'Did Raúl tell you that he was silent for a year?' She

watched as Estelle's already pale face drained of colour. 'We did not know what happened that day, for Raúl could not tell us. The trauma of being trapped with his dead mother...'

'How long were they trapped for?'

'For the night,' Angela said. 'They went over a cliff. It would seem Gabriella died on impact. When the *médicos* got there he was still begging her to wake up. He kept telling her he was sorry. Once they released him he said nothing for more than a year. How could we take him from his home, from his bed? How could we tell him there was a brother?'

'Excuse me—'

Estelle retched and cried into the toilet, and then tried to hold it together. Raúl did not need her drama today. So she rinsed her mouth and combed her hair, then headed back just as Raúl was coming out from the lounge.

'Are you okay?'

'Of course.'

'My father is going to have a rest. As you heard, my brother is coming for dinner tonight. I have agreed that we will stay.'

Estelle nodded.

'Somehow we will get through dinner without killing each other, and then,' Raúl said, 'as my reward for behaving...' He smiled and pulled her in, whispered something crude in her ear.

Far from being offended, Estelle smiled and then whispered into *his* ear. 'I can do it now if you want.'

She felt him smile on her cheek, a little shocked by her response.

'It can wait.' He kissed her cheek. 'Thank you for today. Without you I would not be here.'

'How is he?'

'Frail…sick…'

'He loves you.'

'I know,' Raúl said. 'And because I love him also, we will get through tonight.'

She wasn't so sure they'd get through it when she met Luka. He was clearly going through the motions just for the sake of his parents. Angela was setting up dinner in the garden and Antonio was sitting in the lounge. It was Estelle who got there first, and opened the door as Raúl walked down the hall.

The camera did not lie: he was a younger version of Raúl—and an angrier one too.

Luka barely offered a greeting, just walked into his family home where it seemed there were now two bulls in the same paddock. He refused Raúl's hand when he held it out to him and cussed and then spoke in rapid Spanish.

'What did he say?' Estelle asked as Luka strode through.

'Something about the prodigal son's homecoming and to save the acting for in front of his father.'

'Come on,' Estelle said. There would be time for dwelling on it later.

He caught her wrist. 'You're earning your keep tonight.'

He saw the grit of her teeth and the flash of her eyes.

'Do you do it deliberately, Raúl?' she asked 'Does it help to remind me of my place on a night like tonight?'

'I am sorry. What I meant was that things are particularly strained. When I asked you I never anticipated bringing you here. Certainly I never thought I would set foot in this house.'

They could not discuss it properly here, so for now she gave him the benefit of the doubt. They went out to the garden, where Luka was talking with his father, and they all sat at the table for what should have been a most difficult dinner. Instead, for the most part, it was nice. It was little uncomfortable at first, but soon conversation was flowing as Estelle helped Angela to bring out the food.

'I never thought I would see this day,' Antonio said. 'My family all at the same table…'

Antonio would never see it again.

He was so frail and weak it was clear this would be the last time. It was for that reason, perhaps, that Luka and Raúl attempted to be amicable.

'You work in Bilbao?' Raúl asked.

'I do,' Luka said. 'Investment banking.'

'I had heard of you even before this,' Raúl said. 'You are making a name for yourself.'

'And you.' Luka smiled but it did not meet his eyes. 'I hear about your many acquisitions…'

Thank God for morphine, Estelle thought, because Antonio just smiled and did not pick up on the tension.

The food was amazing—a mixture of dishes from the north and south of Spain. There was *pringá*, an Andalusian dish that was a slow-cooked mixture of meats and had been Raúl's favourite as a child. And there was *marmitako* too, a dish from the Basque Country, which was full of potatoes and pimientos and, Antonio said, had kept him going for so long.

'So you study?' Antonio said to Estelle.

'Ancient architecture.' Estelle nodded. 'Although, I haven't been doing much lately.'

'Yes, what happened to your online studies?' Raúl teased.

'Sol's happened.' Estelle smiled.

Raúl laughed. 'Being married to me is a full-time job…'

Raúl used the words she had used about Gordon. It was a gentle tease, a joke that caused a ripple of laughter—

except their eyes met for a brief moment and it hurt her that he was speaking the truth.

It *was* a job, Estelle reminded herself. A job that would soon be over. But then she thought of the life that grew inside her, the baby that must have the two most mismatched parents in the world.

Not that Raúl knew it.

He thought she loved the clubs and the parties, whereas sitting and eating with his family, as difficult as it was, was where she would rather be. This night, for Estelle, was one of the best.

'You would love San Sebastian.' Antonio carried on speaking to her. 'The architecture is amazing. Raúl, you should take Estelle and explore with her. Take her to the Basilica of Santa Maria—there is so much she would love to see…'

'Estelle would prefer to go out dancing at night. Anyway,' Raúl quipped, 'I haven't been inside a church for years.'

'You will be inside one soon,' his father warned. 'And you should share in your wife's interests.'

Estelle watched thankfully as Raúl took a drink rather than delivering a smart response to his father's marital advice.

And, as much as she'd love to explore the amazing city, she and Raúl were simply too different. And the most bizarre thing was Raúl didn't even know that they were.

She tried to imagine a future: Raúl coming home from a night out to a crying baby, or to nannies, or having access weekends. And she tried to picture the life she would have to live in Spain if she wanted his support.

Estelle remembered the menace in his voice when he had warned that he didn't want children and decided then that she would never tell him while this contract was between them. When she was back home in England and there was distance, when she could tell him without breaking down, or hang up on him if she was about to, *then* she would confess.

And there would be no apology either. Estelle surged in sudden defensiveness for her child—she wasn't going to start its life by apologising for its existence. However Raúl dealt with the news was up to him.

'So...' Still Antonio was focused on Estelle. 'You met last year?'

'We did.' Estelle smiled.

'When he said he was seeing an ex, I thought it was that...' Antonio snapped his fingers. 'The one with the strange name. The one he really liked.'

'Antonio.' Angela chided, but he was too doped up on morphine for inhibition.

'Araminta!' Antonio said suddenly.

'Ah, yes, Araminta.' Estelle smiled sweetly to her husband. 'Was that the one making a play for you at Donald's wedding?'

'That's the one.' Raúl actually looked uncomfortable.

'You were serious for a long time,' Antonio commented.

Estelle glanced up, saw a black smile on Luka's face.

'Weren't you engaged to her?' he asked. 'I remember my mother saying that she thought there might soon be a wedding.'

'Luka,' Angela warned. 'Raúl's wife is here.'

'It's fine,' Estelle attempted—except her cheeks were on fire. She was as jealous as if she had just found out about a bit of her husband's past she'd neither known of nor particularly liked. 'If I'd needed to know about all of Raúl's past before I married him we'd barely have got to his twenties by now.'

She should have left it there, but there was a white-hot

feeling tearing up her throat when she thought of how he'd so cruelly dismissed Araminta—and that was someone he'd once cared about.

It was for that reason her words were tart when she shot Raúl a look. 'Though you failed to mention you'd ever been engaged.'

'We were never engaged.'

'Please!'

Antonio's crack of laughter caught them all by surprise and he raised a glass to Estelle. 'Finally you have met your match.'

It wasn't a long night. Antonio soon tired, and as they headed inside Luka farewelled his father fondly. But the look he gave to Estelle and Raúl told them both he didn't need them to see him to the door in *his* home.

They headed for bed. Estelle was a bit embarrassed by her earlier outburst, especially as everyone else seemed to have managed to behave well tonight.

'I'm sorry about earlier,' she said as she undressed and climbed into bed. 'I shouldn't have said anything about Araminta.'

'You did well,' Raúl said. 'My father actually believes us now.'

He thought she had been acting, Estelle realised. But she hadn't been.

It felt very different sleeping in his father's home from sleeping in Raúl's apartment or on his yacht. Even Raúl's ardour was tempered, and for the first time since she had married him Estelle put on her glasses and pulled out a book. It was the same book she had been reading the day she had met him, about the mausoleum of the First Qin Emperor.

She was still on the same page.

As soon as this was over she was going to focus on

her studies. It had been impossible even to attempt online learning with Raúl around.

'Read me the dirty bits,' Raúl said, and when she didn't comment he took the book from her and looked at the title. 'Well, that will keep it down.'

For his effort he got a half smile.

'You really like all that stuff?'

'I do.'

His hand was on her hip, stroking slowly down. 'They should hear us arguing now,' he teased lightly. 'You demanding details about my past.'

'I don't need to know.'

'My time in Scotland was amazing.' Raúl spoke on regardless. 'I shared a house with Donald and a couple of others. For the first time since my mother died I had one bedroom, one home, a group of friends. We had wild times but it was all good. Then I met Araminta, we started going out, and I guess it was as close to love as I have ever come. But, no, we were never engaged.'

'I really don't need to hear about it.' She turned to him angrily. 'Do you remember the way you spoke to her?' She struggled to keep her voice down. 'The way you treated her?' She looked at his black eyes, imagined running into him a few years from now and being flicked away like an annoying fly. She wasn't hurting for Araminta, Estelle realised. She was hurting for herself—for a time in her future without him.

'So, should I have slept with her as she requested?'

'No!'

'Should I have danced with her when she asked?'

Estelle hated that he was right.

'Anyway, we were never engaged. Her father looked down on me because I didn't come with some inherited title, so I ended things.'

'You dumped her for that?'

'She was lucky I gave a reason,' Raúl said.

Estelle let out a tense breath—he could be so arrogant and cold at times.

'Normally I don't.'

She returned to her book, tried to pick up where she had left off. Just as she would try to pick up her life in a few weeks' time. Except now everything had changed.

'Put down the book,' Raúl said.

'I'm reading.'

'You are the slowest reader I have ever met,' Raúl teased. 'If we ever watch a movie with subtitles we will have to pause every frame.'

She gave up pretending to read, and as she took off her glasses and put down the book he was suddenly serious.

'Not that we will be watching many more movies.'

She lay on her pillow and faced him.

'I could not have done this without you,' Raúl said. 'I nearly didn't come here in time.' He brushed her hair back from his face with her hand.

'You made it, though.'

'It will be over soon.' He looked into her eyes and didn't know if he was dreading his father dying or that soon she would be gone. 'You'll be back to your studies…'

'And you'll be back on your yacht, partying along the coastline.'

'We could maybe go out on the yacht this weekend?' Was he starting to think of her in ways that he had sworn not to? Or was he simply not thinking straight, given that he was here? 'We had a good time.'

'We did have a good time,' Estelle said, but then she shook her head, because she was tired of running away from the world with Raúl. 'But can we just leave it at that?'

She did not want to taint the memory—didn't want to

return to the yacht with hope, only to find out that what they had found there no longer existed.

But for one more night it did.

He held her face and kissed her—a very slow kiss that tasted tender. She felt as if they were back on the boat, could almost hear the lap of the water as he pulled her closer to him and wrapped her in his arms, urged her to join him in one final escape.

Estelle did.

She kissed him as though she were his wife in more than name. She kissed him as though they were really the family they were pretending to be, sharing and loving each other through difficult times.

He had never known a kiss like it; her hands were in his hair, her mouth was one with his, their bodies were meshing, so familiar with each other now. And he wanted her in his bed for ever.

'Estelle….' He was on the edge of saying something he must not, so he made love to her instead.

His hands roamed her body; he kissed her hard as he slid inside her. Side on, they faced each other as he moved and neither closed their eyes.

'Estelle?'

He said it again. It was a question now—a demand to know how she felt. She could feel him building inside her but she was holding back—not on her orgasm. She was holding back on telling him how she felt. They were making love and they both knew it, though neither dared to admit it.

She stared at this man who had her heart. She didn't even need to kiss him to feel his mouth, because deep inside he consumed her. She was pressing her hips into him, her orgasm so low and intense that he moaned as she gripped him. He closed his eyes as he joined her, then forced them open just to watch the blush on her cheeks, the grimace on her face, just to see the face he loved come to him.

She knew he would turn away from her afterwards. Knew they had taken things too far, that there had been true tenderness.

She looked at the scar on his back and waited till dawn for his breathing to quicken, for Raúl to awake abruptly and take her as he did most mornings.

It never happened.

CHAPTER SIXTEEN

HE WOKE AND he waited for reason.

For relief to flood in because he had held back his words last night.

It never came.

He turned and watched her awaken. He should be bored by now. She should annoy him by now.

'What am I thinking?' he asked when she opened her eyes and smiled at him.

'I wouldn't presume to know.'

'I *did* meet you that night,' he said. 'Despite the dress and the make-up, it *was* Estelle.'

He was getting too close for comfort. Raúl had never been anything other than himself. She, on the other hand, changed at every turn—he didn't actually know her at all. Sex was their only true form of communication.

Estelle could hear noises from the kitchen and was relieved to have a reason to leave. 'I'll go and give Angela a hand.' She went to climb out of bed, wondering if she should say anything about what Angela had told her last night. 'I spoke to her yesterday...'

'Later,' Raúl said, and she nodded.

Today was already going to be painful enough.

* * *

'Buenos días,' Raúl greeted Angela.

'Buenos días.' Angela smiled. 'I was just making your father his breakfast. What would you like?'

'Don't worry about us,' Raúl said. 'We'll have some coffee and then Estelle and I might go for a walk.'

'What time are you going back?'

'I'm not sure,' Raúl said. 'Maybe we might stay a bit longer?'

'That would be good,' Angela said. 'Why don't you take your father's tray in and tell him?'

He was in there for ages, and Angela and Estelle shared a look when at one point they heard laughter.

'I am so glad that they have had this time,' Angela said, and then Raúl came out, and he and Estelle headed off for a walk along the sweeping hillsides on his father's property.

'Have you been here before?' Estelle asked. 'To San Sebastian, I mean?'

'A couple of times,' Raúl said. 'Would you like to explore?'

'We're here to spend time with your father,' Estelle said, nervous about letting her façade down, admitting just how much she would like to.

'I guess,' Raúl said. 'But, depending on how long we stay, I am sure the newlyweds would like some private time too.'

'Wouldn't you be bored?'

'If I am I can wait in the gift shop.' Raúl smiled, and so did she, and then he told her some of what he had been talking about with his father. 'He has told my aunt and uncle about Angela and Luka.'

'When?'

'Yesterday. When he knew I was on my way,' Raúl said. 'He didn't want to leave it to me to tell them.'

'How did they take it?'

'He asked if we heard any shouting while we were flying up.' Raúl gave a small mirthless laugh. 'They want him dead, of course. He told them they wouldn't have long to wait.'

They walked for ages, hardly talking, and Raúl was comfortable with silence, because he was trying to think—trying to work out if she even wanted to hear what he was about to ask her.

'You miss England?'

'I do,' Estelle said. 'Well, I miss my family.'

'Will you miss me?' He stopped walking.

She turned to him and didn't know how to respond. 'I won't miss the clubs and the restaurants...'

'Will you miss *us*?'

'I can't give the right answer here.'

'You can.' He took her in his arms. 'You were right. I miss out on so much...'

It was a fragile admission, she could feel that, and she was scared to grasp it in case somehow it dispersed. But she could not deny her feelings any longer. 'You don't have to.'

His mouth was on hers and they were kissing as if for the first time—a teenage kiss as they paused in the hills, a kiss that had nothing to do with business; a kiss that had nothing to do with sex. His fingers were moving into her hair, touching her face as if he were blind, and she was a whisper away from telling him, from confessing the truth. Just so they could tell his father—just so there might be one less regret.

'Raúl...'

He looked into her eyes and she thought she could tell him anything when he looked at her like that. But for the moment she held back. Because a child was something far bigger than this relationship they were almost exploring. She remembered her vow to do this well away from their contract.

'Let's get back.'

They walked down the hill hand in hand, talking about nothing in particular—about France, so close, and the drive they could maybe take tomorrow, or the next day. They were just a couple walking, heading back home to their family—and then she felt his hand tighten on hers.

'It's the *médico*.'

They ran the remaining distance, though he paused for just a moment to collect himself before they pushed open the front door. Because even from there they could hear the sound of Angela sobbing.

'Your father...' Angela stumbled down the hall and Raúl held her as she wept into his arms. 'He has passed away.'

CHAPTER SEVENTEEN

ESTELLE COULDN'T BELIEVE how quickly things happened.

Luka arrived soon after, and spent time with his father. But it was clear he did not appreciate having Raúl and Estelle in his home.

'Stay,' Angela said.

'We'll go to a hotel.'

'Please, Raúl…'

Estelle's heart went out to her, but it was clear that Luka did not want them there and so they spent the night in a small hotel. Raúl was pensive and silent.

The next morning they stood in the small church to say farewell. The two brothers stood side by side, but they were not united in their grief.

'I used to think Luka was the chosen one,' Raúl said as they flew late that afternoon back to Marbella for the will to be read, as per his father's wishes. 'When I found out—when my father said he wanted to die there—I felt his other family were the real ones.' His eyes met hers. 'Luka sees things differently. He was a secret—his father's shame. I got to work alongside him. I was the reason he did not see much of his father when he was small. His hatred runs deep.'

'Does yours?'

'I don't know,' Raúl admitted. 'I don't know how I feel. I just want to get the reading of the will over with.'

It wasn't a pleasant gathering. Paola and Carlos were there, and the look they gave Angela as she walked in was pure filth.

'She doesn't need this—' Estelle started, but Raúl shot her a look.

'It was never going to be nice,' he said.

Estelle bit her lip, and tried to remember her opinion on his family was not what she was here for. But she kept remembering the night they had made love, their walk on the hill the next morning, and tried to hold on to a love that had almost been there—she was sure of it.

She sat silent beside him as the will was read, heard the low murmurs as the lawyer spoke with Angela. From her limited Spanish, Estelle could make out that she was keeping the home in San Sebastian and there were also some investments that had been made in her name.

And then he addressed Luka.

Estelle heard a shocked gasp from Paola and Carlos and then a furious protest started. But Raúl sat still and silent and said nothing.

'What's happening?'

He didn't answer her.

As the room finally settled the lawyer addressed Raúl. He gave a curt nod, then stood.

'Come on.'

He took her by the arm and they walked out.

Angela followed, calling to him. 'Raúl…'

'Don't.' He shrugged her off. 'You got what you wanted.'

Estelle had to run to keep up with his long strides, but finally he told her what was happening.

'His share of the business goes to Luka.' His face was grey when he turned and faced her. 'Even dying still he plays games, still he lies.' He shook his head. 'I get a vine-yard…'

'Raúl,' Angela had caught up with them. 'He saw how happy you two were the night before he died.'

'He did not change his will.'

'No, but it was his dream that his two sons would work side by side together.'

'He should have thought about that twenty-five years ago.'

'Raúl…'

But Raúl was having none of it. He strode away from Angela and all too soon they were back in his apartment and rapid decisions were being made.

'I'll sell my share,' he said. 'I will start again.' He would. Raúl had no qualms about starting again. 'And I will sell that vineyard too…'

'Why?'

'Because I don't want it,' he said. 'I don't want anything from *him*. I don't want to build bridges with my brother.' *His* mother's business was being handed over to her husband's illegitimate son—it would kill her if she wasn't dead already.

Raúl was back in the mountains—could hear her furious shouts and screams, the storm raging; he could hear the screech of tyres and the scrape of metal. He was over the cliff again. But that part he could manage—that part he could deal with. It was next part he dreaded.

It was the silence after that, and he would do anything never to hear it again.

'You don't have to make any decisions tonight. We can talk about it—'

'We?' His lips tore into a savage smile. '*We* will talk about *my* future? Estelle, I think *you* are forgetting your place.'

'No.' She refused to deny it any longer. 'The morning your father died, when were talking, we were *both* choosing to forget my place. If you want a relationship you can't pick and choose the times!'

'A relationship?' He stared at her for the longest time.

'Yes,' Estelle said, and she was the bravest she had ever been. 'A relationship. I think that's what you want.'

'Now she tells me what I want? You *love* me, do you? You *care* about me, do you? Have you any idea how boring that is to hear? I *bought* you so we could avoid this very conversation. You'd do well to remember that.'

Estelle just stood there as he stormed out of the apartment. She didn't waste her breath warning him this time.

She refused to be his keeper.

CHAPTER EIGHTEEN

RAÚL SAT IN Sol's with the music pumping and stared at the heaving dance floor.

A vineyard.

A vineyard which, if he sold it, wouldn't even pay for his yacht for a year—would Estelle stick around then?

Yes.

He had never doubted his ability to start again, but he doubted it now—could not bear the thought of letting her down.

'Te odio.' He could hear his five-year-old voice hurling the words at his mother, telling her he hated her for missing his play.

He'd been a child, a five-year-old having a row, yet for most of his life he had thought those words had driven his mother to despair that day.

Could he do it?

Whisk Estelle away from a family that loved her to live in the hills with a man who surely wasn't capable of love?

Except he did love her.

And she loved him.

He had done everything he could think of to ensure it would not happen, had put so many rules in place, and yet here it was—staring at him, wrapping around him like a blanket on a stifling day.

He did not want her love, did not want the weight of it. Did not want to be responsible for another's heart.

She would stand by him, Raúl knew, but the fallout was going to be huge. The empire was divided. He could smell the slash and burn that would take place and he did not want her exposed to it.

His phone buzzed in his pocket but he refused to look at it, because if he saw her name he would weaken.

Raúl looked across the dance floor, saw an upper-class hooker, ordered her a drink and gestured her over.

He took out some money and as she opened her bag made his request.

'Lápiz de labios,' Raúl said, and pointed to his neck.

He did not have to explain himself to her. She delivered his request—put her mouth to his neck and did as he asked.

'Perfume,' he ordered next, and she took out her cheap scent and sprayed him.

'Gracias.'

It was done now.

Raúl stood and headed for home.

CHAPTER NINETEEN

'AMANDA.' ESTELLE ATTEMPTED to sound normal when she answered the landline. She was staring at the picture of them on Donald's wedding night, trying to fathom the man who simply refused to love.

'I tried your mobile.'

'Sorry…' Estelle had started to talk about the charger she'd left in San Sebastian, started to talk about little things that weren't important at all, when she realised that for once Amanda wasn't being upbeat. 'What's happened?'

'I tried to ring Raúl—I wanted him to break the news to you.'

Estelle felt her heart turn to ice.

'We're at the hospital and the doctors say that they're going to operate tomorrow.'

'Has she put on any weight?'

'She's lost some,' Amanda said. 'But if they don't operate we're going to lose her anyway.'

'I'm coming home.'

'Please…'

'How's Andrew?'

'He's with her now. He's actually been really good. He's sure she's going to make it through.'

'She will.'

'I don't think so,' Amanda admitted, and her sister-in-law who was always so strong, always so positive, finally broke down.

Estelle said everything she could to comfort her, but knew they were only words, that she needed to be there.

'I'm going to hang up now and book a flight,' Estelle told her. 'And I'll try and sort out my phone.'

'Don't worry about the phone,' Amanda said. 'Just get here.'

Estelle grabbed her case and started piling clothes in. Getting to the airport and onto a flight was her aim, but the thought of Cecelia, so small and so weak, undergoing something so major was just too overwhelming and it made Estelle suddenly fold over. She sobbed as she never had before—knew that she had to get the tears out now, so she could be strong for Amanda and Andrew.

Raúl heard her tears as he walked through the apartment and could not stand how much he had hurt her—could not bear that *he* had done this.

'Estelle…' He saw the case and knew that she was leaving.

'Don't worry.' She didn't even look at him. 'The tears aren't for you. Cecelia has been taken back into hospital. They can't wait for the surgery any longer…' She thought of her again, so tiny, and of what would happen to her parents if they lost her. The tears started again. 'I need to get back to them.'

'I'll fix it now.'

He couldn't *not* hold her.

Could not stand the thought of her facing this on her own, not being there beside her.

He held her in his arms and she wept.

And he could not fight it any more for he loved her.

'We'll go now.'

'No.' She was trying to remember that she was angry, but it felt so good to be held.

'Estelle, I've messed up, but I know what I want now. *I know...*'

She smelt it then—the cheap musky scent; she felt it creep into her nostrils. She moved out of his arms and looked at him properly, smelt the whisky on his breath and saw the lipstick on his neck.

'It's not what you think,' Raúl said.

'You're telling me what I think, are you?' Oh, she didn't need him to teach her to cuss in Spanish! 'You win, Raúl!' Her expression revealed her disgust. 'I'm out of here!'

The tears stopped. They weren't for him anyway. She just turned and went on filling her case.

'Estelle—'

'I don't want to hear it, Raúl.' She didn't even raise her voice.

'Okay, not now. We will speak about it on the plane.'

'You're not coming with me, Raúl.'

'Your brother will think it strange if I do not support you.'

'I'm sure my brother has other things on his mind.' She looked at him, dishevelled and unshaven, and scorned him with her eyes. 'Don't make this worse for me, Raúl.'

He went to grab her arm, to stop her.

'Don't touch me!'

He heard her shout, heard the pain—not just for what was going on with her niece, but for the agony of the betrayal she perceived.

'You can't leave like this. You're upset...'

'I'm upset about my niece!' She looked at him. 'I would *never* cry like this over a man who doesn't love me.' She didn't care how much she hurt him now. 'I'm not your mother, Raúl, I'm not going fall apart, or drive over a cliff-edge because the man I'm married to is a cheat. I'm far stronger than that.'

She was.

'All I want now is to get home to my niece.'

He'd lost her. Raúl knew that. Arguing would be worse than futile, for she needed to be with her family urgently.

'I will call my driver and organise a plane.'

'I can sort out transport myself.' Tears for him were starting now, and she didn't want Raúl to see—love was not quite so black and white.

'If you take my plane it will get you there sooner,' Raúl said.

And it would get her away from him before she broke down—before she told him about the baby…before she weakened.

It was the only reason she said yes.

CHAPTER TWENTY

RAÚL STOOD IN the silence.

It was the sound he hated most in the world.

It was his nightmare.

Only this was one *he* had created.

The scent that filled his nostrils was not leaking fuel and death but the scent of cheap perfume and the absence of *her*.

He wanted to chase Estelle—except he was not foolish enough to get in a car, and he could not follow her as his driver was taking her to the airport.

Raúl called a taxi, but even as he climbed in he knew she would not want him with her on the flight. Knew he would be simply delaying her in getting to where she needed to be. They passed De La Fuente Holdings and he looked up, trying to imagine it without his father and Angela, and with Luka working there. Trying to fathom a future that right now he could not see.

Noticing a light on, he asked the driver to stop…

'Raúl!'

Angela tried not to raise her eyes as a very dishevelled Raúl appeared from the elevator.

He was unshaven, his eyes bloodshot. His hair was a mess, and there was lipstick on his collar…

It was the Raúl she knew well.

'What are you doing here at this time, Raúl?'

'I saw the light on,' Raúl said. 'Estelle's niece is sick.'

'I am sorry to hear that. Where is Estelle?'

'Flying back to London.'

'You should be with her, then.' Angela refused to mince her words. He might not want to hear what she had to say to him—he could leave if that were the case.

'She didn't want me to go.'

'So you hit the clubs and picked up a *puta*?'

'No.'

'Don't lie to me, Raúl,' Angela said. 'Your wife would never wear cheap perfume like that.'

'I wouldn't cheat on her. I couldn't.'

Angela paused. Really, the evidence was clear—and yet she knew Raúl better than most and he did not lie. Raúl never attempted to defend the inexcusable.

'So what happened?' Angela asked.

He closed his eyes in shame.

'You know, when you live as a mistress apparently you lose the right to an opinion on others—but of course you have them.' Harsh was the look she gave Raúl. 'Over and over I question your morals.'

'Over and over I do too,' Raúl admitted. 'She got too close.'

'That's what couples do.'

'I did not cheat. I wanted her to think that I had.'

'So now she does.' Angela looked at him. 'So now she's on her own, dealing with her family.'

Angela watched his eyes fill with tears and she tried not to love him as a son, tried not to forgive when she should not. But when he told her what had happened, told her what he had done, the filthy place his head had been, she believed him.

'You push away everyone who loves you. What are you scared of, Raúl?'

'This,' Raúl admitted. 'Hurting another, being responsible for another...'

'We are responsible for ourselves,' Angela said. 'I have made mistakes. Now I pay for them. Now I have till the morning to clear out my office. Now your aunt and uncle turn their backs on me. I would do it all again, though, for the love I had with your father. Some things I would do differently, of course, but I would do it all again.'

'What would you do differently?'

'I would have insisted you were told far sooner about your father and I. I would have told you about your brother,' she said. 'We were going to before you went to university, but your father decided not to at the last moment. I regret that. I should have stood up to him. I should have told you myself. I did not. And I have to live with that. What would *you* have done differently, Raúl?'

'Not have gone to Sol's.' He gave a small smile. 'And many, many other things. But that is the main one now.'

'You need to go to her. You need to tell her what happened—why you did what you did.'

'She doesn't want to hear it,' Raúl said. 'There are more important things on her mind.'

He could not bring himself to tell Angela that their marriage was a fake. If this was fake, then it hurt too much.

And if it was not fake, then it was real.

'If you are not there for her now, with her niece so ill, then it might be too late.'

Raúl nodded. 'She has my plane.'

'I will book you on a commercial flight,' Angela said. 'You need to freshen up.'

He headed to his office, stared in the mirror and picked

up his razor. He called his thanks as she brought him in coffee and a fresh shirt.

'This is the last time I do this for you.'

'Maybe not,' Raúl said. 'Maybe your sons might have a say in that.'

Angela's eyes welled up for a moment as finally he acknowledged the place she had in his heart. But then she met his eyes and told him, 'I meant this is the last time I help you cover up a mistake. Estelle deserves more.'

'She will get it.'

'Your father was so pleased to see how you two were together,' Angela said. 'He was the most peaceful I have ever seen him. He knew he had not allowed time for you and Luka to sort things out, but you are brothers and he believes that will happen. The morning he passed away we were watching you and Estelle walking in the hills. We saw you stop and kiss.'

Raúl closed his eyes as he remembered that day, when for the first time in his life he had been on the edge of admitting love.

'He knew you were happy. I am so glad that I told him about the baby.'

Raúl froze.

'Baby?'

There was no mistaking his bewilderment.

'She has not told you?'

'No!' Raúl could not take it in. 'She told *you*?'

'No,' Angela said. 'I just knew. She did not have any wine; she was sick in the morning…'

Yes, Estelle was tough.

Yes, she could do this without him.

He did not want her to.

'Book the flight.'

CHAPTER TWENTY-ONE

'Raúl!'

The only possible advantage to being in the midst of a family crisis was that no one noticed the snap to her voice or the tension on Estelle's features when a clean-shaven, lipstick-free Raúl walked in.

'I'm sorry I couldn't get here sooner.' He shook Andrew's hand.

'No, we're grateful to you for getting Estelle here,' Andrew said. 'We're very sorry about your father.'

It was strange, but in a crisis it was Andrew who was the strong one. Amanda barely looked up.

'Is she in surgery?' Raúl sat down next to Estelle and put his arm around her. He felt her shoulders stiffen.

'An hour ago.' Her words were stilted. 'It could be several hours yet.'

The clock ticked on.

Raúl read every poster on the wall and every pamphlet that was laid out. She could hear the turning of the pages and it only served to irritate her. Why on earth had he come? Why couldn't she attempt to get over him with him still far away?

'Why won't they give us an update?' asked Amanda's mother. 'It's ridiculous that they don't let us know what's going on.'

'They will soon,' Andrew said, and Raúl watched as Andrew put his arm around his wife and comforted her, saw how she leant on him, how much she needed him.

Despite everything.

Because of everything, Raúl realised.

'Why don't you wait in the hotel?' Estelle suggested when she could not stand him being in the room a moment longer. 'I've got a room there.'

'I want to wait with you.'

He headed out to the vending machine and she followed him. 'I need some change,' he said. 'I haven't got any pounds.'

'Why would you make this worse for me?'

'I'm not trying to make it worse for you,' Raúl said. 'I know this is neither the time nor the place, but you need to know that nothing happened except my asking a woman to kiss my neck and spray me with her perfume.' He looked her right in the eye. 'I wanted you gone.'

'Well, it worked.'

'I made a mistake,' Raúl said. 'The most foolish of mistakes. I did not want to put you through what was to come.'

'Shouldn't that be *my* choice?' She looked at him.

'Yes,' he said simply. 'As it should be mine.'

Estelle didn't understand his response, was in no mood for cryptic games, and she shook her head in frustration. She wanted him gone and yet she wanted him here— wanted to forgive, to believe.

'I can't do this now,' Estelle said. 'Right now I have to concentrate on my niece.'

As much as Raúl longed to be there for her, that much he understood. 'Do you want me to wait in the hotel or stay with you here?'

'The hotel,' Estelle said—because she could not think straight with him around, could not keep her thoughts where they needed to be with Raúl by her side. She wanted his arms around her, wanted the comfort only he could give, and yet she could not stand what he had done.

'Could I get a coffee as well?' Andrew wheeled himself over.

'Of course,' Raúl said as Estelle handed him some change.

'Estelle, could you take Amanda for a walk?' Andrew asked. 'Just get her away from the waiting room. Her parents are driving her crazy, asking how much longer it will be.'

'Sure.'

Estelle's eyes briefly met Raúl's, warning him to be gone by the time she returned, and Raúl knew the fight he had on his hands. He watched as Estelle suggested a walk to Amanda and he saw a family in motion, supporting each other, a family that was there for each other. A family who helped, who fixed—or tried to.

He looked to Andrew. 'You have the best sister in the world.'

'I know,' Andrew said. 'I'd do anything for her.'

As would Estelle for him, Raúl thought. She'd sold her soul to the devil for her family, but now he understood why.

'I am going to wait in the hotel,' Raúl said. 'I didn't sleep at all last night.'

'I know.' Andrew nodded. 'I'm sure Estelle will keep you up to date.'

'What hotel is she staying at?'

'Over the road,' Andrew told him. 'Good luck—I'm sure it's not at all what you're used to.'

'It will be fine.'

'You just wait.' Andrew gave a pale smile. 'I had to wait fifteen minutes just for them to find a ramp.'

They chatted on for a while—Andrew trying to keep

his mind out of the surgery, Raúl simply because Andrew wanted to talk.

'I had my reservations about the two of you at first,' Andrew admitted. 'You're so opposite.'

And then Raúl found out from his wife's brother just how much Estelle hated clubs and bars, found out exactly the lengths she had gone to for her family.

There was one length she would not go to, though. Raúl was certain of that now.

He walked alongside Andrew's chair, down long corridors, past the operating theatres and Intensive Care, and back again a few times over—until he saw Estelle returning and knew it was better for her that he leave.

He paced the small hotel room, waiting for news—because surely it was taking too long. It was now nine p.m., and he was sick to his stomach for a baby he had never met and a family he wanted to be a part of.

'She made it through surgery.'

Raúl could hear both the relief and the strain in Estelle's voice when the door opened.

'When did she get out of Theatre?'

'About six.' She glanced over to him. 'Was I supposed to ring and inform you?'

He could hear the sarcasm in her voice. 'I just thought it was taking too long. I thought…'

'I'm sorry.' Estelle regretted her sarcastic response—she could see the concern on his face was genuine. 'It was just a long wait till they let Andrew and Amanda in to see her. They've only just been allowed.'

'How is she?'

'Still here.' Estelle peeled off her clothes. 'I've lost my phone charger. I gave Andrew your number in case anything happens overnight.'

It was, though she would never admit it, a relief to have him here, to know that if the phone rang in the night he would be the one to answer it. It was a relief, too, to sink into bed and close her eyes, but there was something that needed to be dealt with before the bliss of sleep.

'I'm not going to tell them we're over yet,' Estelle said. 'It would be too much for them to deal with now. But after we visit in the morning can you make your excuses and leave.'

'I want to be here.'

'I don't want you here, though, and given what's happened you don't own me any more.' She stared into the dark. 'Exclusive, remember?'

'I've told you—nothing happened,' Raúl said. 'Which means I do still own you.'

'No,' Estelle said, 'you don't. Because whatever went on I've decided that I don't want your money. It costs too much.'

'Then pay me back.'

'I will…' she attempted, but of course a considerable amount had already been spent. 'I fully intend to pay you back. It just might take some time.'

'Whatever you choose. But it changes nothing now, Estelle…' He reached for her, wanted to speak with her, but she shrugged him off and turned to her side.

'I'd like the night off.'

'Granted.'

She woke in his arms and wriggled away from them, and then rang her brother. Raúl watched as she went to climb out of bed, saw the extra heaviness to her breasts and the darkening pink of her areolae, and he loved her all the more for not telling him, for guarding their child from the contract that had once bound them. It was the only leverage he had.

'You'll leave after visiting?' Estelle checked.

'Why would I leave my wife at a time like this?' Raúl asked. 'I'm not going anywhere, Estelle.'

'I don't want you here.'

'I don't believe you,' Raúl said. 'I believe you love me as much as I love you.'

'Love you!' Estelle said. 'I'd be mad to love you.' She shook her head. 'You might have almost sent me crazy once, Raúl, but if I possibly did love you then it's gone. My love has conditions too, and you didn't adhere to them. I don't care about technicalities, Raúl. Even if you didn't sleep with someone else, what you did was wrong.'

'Then we go back to the contract.' He caught her wrist. 'Which means I dictate the terms.'

'Your father's dead. Surely it's over?'

'We agreed on a suitable pause. You should read things more closely before you sign them, Estelle.' He watched her shoulders rise and fall. 'But I agree it has proved more complicated than either of us could have anticipated. For that reason, I will agree that the contract expires tomorrow.'

'Tomorrow?' Estelle asked. 'Why not now?'

'I just want one more night. And if I have to exercise the terms of the contract to speak with you—believe me, I shall.'

CHAPTER TWENTY-TWO

'SHE'S PINK!'

Estelle couldn't believe the little pink fingers that wrapped around hers. Even Cecelia's nails were pink—it was suddenly her favourite colour in the world.

'That's the first thing we said.' Andrew was holding Cecelia's other hand. 'She's been fighting so much since the day she was born.' Andrew smiled down at his daughter.

All were too entranced by the miracle that was Cecelia to notice how much Raúl was struggling.

Raúl looked down at the infant, who resembled Estelle, and could hardly believe what he had almost turned his back on.

'I have to go and do some work,' Raúl said. 'Do you want to get lunch later?'

Estelle looked up, about to say no, but he was talking to Andrew.

'Just at the canteen,' he added.

'That would be great.' Andrew smiled. 'Estelle, could you take Amanda for some breakfast? She wants one of us with Cecelia all the time but she needs to get out of the unit and get some fresh air.'

'Sure.' Estelle stood.

'I thought we could go for dinner tonight.'

This time Raúl *was* speaking to Estelle.

'I'm here to be with my niece.'

'Andrew and Amanda are with her. As long as she continues to improve I am sure they expect you to eat.'

'Of course we do,' Andrew said. 'Go out tonight, Estelle. You need a break from the hospital too!'

It was a long day. The doctors were in and out with Cecelia, and talked about taking her breathing tube out if she continued to hold her own. Amanda's parents went home, to return at the weekend, and after they had gone Estelle finally persuaded Amanda to have a sleep in one of the parents' rooms.

It was exhausting.

As she closed the door and went to head back to Cecelia she wondered if she had, after all, grown far too used to Raúl's lifestyle—she would have given anything to be back on his yacht, just drifting along, with nothing to think about other than what the next meal might be and how long it would be till they made love again.

Being Raúl's tart hadn't all been bad, Estelle thought with a wry smile as she returned to Cecelia.

It was being his wife that was hell.

'Amanda's asleep,' Estelle said. 'Well, for a little while.'

'Thanks for being here for us,' Andrew said. 'Both of you. Raúl's great. I admit I wasn't sure at first, but you can see how much he cares for you.'

She felt tears prick her eyes,

'Did you ask him to offer me a job?'

'A job?'

She couldn't lie easily to her brother, but instantly he knew that Estelle's surprised response was real, that she'd had no idea.

'Raúl said that when things are sorted with Cecelia there will be a job waiting for me. He wants me to check out his hotels, work on adjustments for the disabled. There will be a lot of travel, and it will be tough being away at first. But once Cecelia's better he says we can broaden things so it's not just about travelling with disabilities but with a young child as well.'

It was a dream job. She could see it in her brother's eyes. Soon he would be earning, travelling, and more than that his self-respect and confidence would start to return.

'It sounds wonderful.' Estelle gave him a hug, but though she smiled and said the right thing she was furious with Raúl—his company was about to implode, and she and Raúl were soon to divorce quietly.

How dared he enmesh himself further? How dared he involve Andrew in the chaos they had made?

She wanted it to be tomorrow, she wanted Raúl gone so she could sort out how she felt, sort out her life, sort out how to tell him that the temporary contract they had signed would, however tentatively, bind them for life.

There was a note from Raúl waiting for her when she reached the hotel, telling her that he was tied up in a meeting but would see her at the restaurant at eight.

'You signed up for this,' Estelle told herself aloud as she put on her eye make-up. She wondered if it would be just dinner, or perhaps a club after, or…

Estelle closed her eyes so sharply that she almost scratched her eyeball with her mascara wand. He surely wouldn't expect them to sleep together?

He surely wouldn't insist?

Then again, Estelle told herself as she took a taxi to the restaurant, this was Raúl.

Of course he would insist.

Worse, though, she knew she must comply—no matter the toll on heart.

* * *

He turned heads. He just did.

He was waiting for her at the bar, and when they walked into the smartest of restaurants he might as well have being stepping out of a helicopter in a kilt—because everybody was looking at him.

'You look beautiful,' Raúl told her as they sat down.

'Thank you,' she said.

He could feel the anger hissing and spitting inside her, guessed that she must have spoken to Andrew since lunchtime.

'It's a lovely dress,' he commented. 'New?'

'I chose it.'

'It suits you.'

'I know.'

He ordered wine. She declined.

He suggested seafood, which he knew she loved, but he had read in one of the many leaflets he perused in the hospital waiting room that pregnant woman were advised not to eat it.

'I thought you loved seafood?' Raúl commented when she refused it, wondering what her excuse would be.

'I've had enough of it.'

She ordered steak, and he watched her slice it angrily before she voiced one of the many things that were on her mind.

'Did you offer my brother a job?'

'I did.'

'Why would you do that? Why would you do that when you're about to walk away? When you know the company's heading for trouble?'

'We're not heading for trouble,' Raúl said. 'I have been speaking with Luka at length today, and Carlos and Paola too. There is to be a name-change. To Sanchez De La

Fuente... Anyway, if there is trouble ahead it will only be in the office. Your brother will not be dealing with it.'

'What about when we divorce? Will you use him as a pawn then?'

'Never. I tell you this: it is a proper offer, and as long as your brother does well he will have a job.'

'You say that now...'

'I always keep my word.' He looked at her. 'I don't lie,' Raúl said. 'From the start I have only been myself.' He watched the colour spread up her cheeks. 'You get the truth, whether you like or not. I think we both know that much about me.'

Reluctantly she nodded.

'It is only wives that I employ on a whim. I am successful because I choose my employees carefully and I don't give out sympathy jobs. Your brother pointed out a few things that could be changed at the hotel. He would like the menu outside the restaurant to be displayed lower too. He said he would not like to find out about the menu and the prices from a woman he was perhaps dating with.'

Estelle gave a reluctant smile. It was the sort of thing Andrew *would* say.

'He said that a lower table at Reception would be a nice touch, so that anyone in a wheelchair could check in there. That means I do not have to refurbish our reception areas. He has saved me more than his year's wage already.'

'Okay.'

'I don't want my hotels to be good, I want them to be the best—and by the best I mean the best for everyone: businessmen, people with families, the disabled. Your brother, as I told him, will soon be all three.' He looked at her for a long moment, wondering if now she might tell him. 'It is good to see Cecelia improving,' Raúl said. 'It must be a huge relief.'

'It is,' Estelle admitted. 'I think we're only now realising just how scary the last few months have been.'

'Does seeing your niece make you consider ever having a baby?'

She gave a cynical laugh.

'It's just about put me off for life, seeing all that they have had to go through.'

'But they've made it.'

She wasn't going to tell him about the baby, Raúl realised. But, far from angering him, it actually made him smile as he sat opposite the strongest woman he knew.

'Here...' At the end of the meal he smeared cream cheese on a cracker, added a dollop of quince paste and handed it to her.

'No, thanks. I'm full.'

'But remember the night we met...'

'I'd rather not.'

He saw tears prick her eyes and went to take her hand. He could not believe all that they had been through in recent weeks. As she pulled her hand away Raúl wasn't so sure they'd survived it.

'I'm sorry for hurting you. I overreacted—thought I was going to lose everything, thought I might not be able to give you the lifestyle—'

'Like I need your yacht,' Estelle spat. 'Like I need to eat out at posh restaurants seven nights a week, or wear the clothes you chose.'

'So if you don't want all that,' Raúl pointed out, 'what *do* you want?'

'Nothing,' Estelle said. 'I want nothing from you.'

He called for the bill and paid, and as they headed out of the restaurant he took her hand and held it tightly. He turned her to him and kissed her.

It tasted of nothing.

He kissed her harder.

She wanted to spit him out. Not because she loathed his mouth but because she wanted to sink into it for ever—wanted to believe his lies, wanted to think for a moment that she could hold him, that he'd want their baby as much as she did, that he'd want the real her if he knew who she was.

'Where now?' Raúl asked. 'I know…' He held her by the hips. 'You could show me Dario's…'

'I didn't meet Gordon at Dario's,' Estelle said. 'I told you that.'

'We could go anyway,' Raúl said. 'It's our last night together, and it sounds like fun.'

He saw the conflict in her eyes, saw her take a breath to force another lie. He would not put her through it, so he kissed her instead.

'Let's get back to the hotel.'

'Raúl…' She just couldn't go through with it—could not keep up the pretence a moment longer, could not bear to be made love to just to have her heart ripped apart again.

'What?' He took her by the hand again, led her to a taxi.

'Come on, Estelle…' He undressed speedily. 'It's been a hell of a day. I would like to come.'

'You can be *so* romantic.'

'But you keep insisting this is not about romance,' Raúl pointed out.

Her face burnt.

'I don't understand what has suddenly changed. We have been having sex for a couple of months now…' He was undoing her zipper, undressing her. He was down on one knee, removing her shoes. 'Tomorrow we are finished. Tonight we celebrate.'

'I don't want you.'

'So you did the other times?' he checked.

At every exit he blocked her. At every turn he made her see it had never been paid sex for her—not for one single second, not for one shared kiss. She had been lying from the very start. For she had loved him from the start.

'Estelle, after tonight you have the rest of the century off where we are concerned.'

He laid her on the bed and kissed her, felt her cold in his arms. His mouth was on her nipple and he swirled it with his tongue then blew on it, watching it stiffen and ripen. Then he took it deep in his mouth, his fingers intimately stroking her. He filled her mouth with his tongue and she just lay there.

This was what she had signed up for, Estelle reminded herself. She didn't have to enjoy it. Except she was.

It was like a guilty secret—a *filthy* guilty secret. Because she wanted him so—wanted him deep inside her. She turned her cheek away but he turned it back and kissed her. She did not respond—or her mouth did its best not to.

He felt the shift in her…kissed her back to him.

He felt the motion of her tongue on his, felt *her*.

'Tell me to stop and I will,' Raúl said.

She just stared at him.

'Tell me…'

She couldn't

'You can't stop this any more than I can…'

He moved up onto his elbows and she tried not to look at him, looked at his shoulder, which moved back and forth over her.

'Tell me…' he said.

She held on.

'Tell me how you feel…'

In a moment she would. In a moment she'd be sobbing

and begging in his arms. She lifted her hips, and then lifted them again, just so she could hurry him along.

'I'm going to come…' she moaned.

'Liar.'

He pushed deeper within her, hit that spot she would rather tonight he did not, for her face was burning, and her hands were roaming, and her hips were lifting with a life of their own as she let out a low, suppressed moan.

She felt a flood of warmth to her groin, felt the insistence of him inside her, the demand that she match his want.

'You couldn't pay for this…' He was stroking her deep inside and seducing her with his words. 'You could never fake this…'

He slipped into Spanish as she left the planet; he toppled onto her and bucked rapidly inside her as she sobbed out her orgasm. She didn't know where she started or ended, didn't know how to handle the love in her heart and the child in her belly. All belonged to the man holding her in his arms.

'You want me just as much as I want you.'

'So?' She stared back at him. 'What does that prove? That you're good in bed?' She turned away from him and curled up like a ball. 'I think you already knew that.'

'It proves that I am right to trust you. That it is nothing to do with contracts or money. That you *do* love me as much as I love you.'

'You don't know me, though.' She started to cry. 'I've been lying all along.'

'I know you far more than you think,' Raúl said.

'You don't. Your father was right. I like churches and reading…'

'I know that.'

'And I hate clubs.'

'I know that too.'

'I'm nothing like the woman you thought you met.'

'Do you not think I'd long ago worked that out?' Raúl kissed her cheek. 'My virgin hooker.'

He heard her gurgle of laughter, born from exhausted tears.

'I don't get how you're the one with no morals, yet I'm the one who's lied.'

'Because you're complicated,' Raúl said. 'Because you're female.' He kissed her mouth. 'Because you loved me from the start.'

She went to object, but he was telling the truth.

'Do you know when I fell in love with you?' Raúl said. 'When I saw you in those tatty pyjamas and I did not want you in Gordon's bed. It had nothing to do with me paying you. I deserved that slap, but you really did misinterpret my words.'

She was so scared to love him, so scared to tell him about the baby. But if they were to survive, if they were to start to trust, then she had to. It never entered her head that he already knew.

'When were you going to tell me you're pregnant, Estelle?'

She felt his hand move to her stomach, felt his kiss on the back of her neck. All she could be was honest now. 'When I was too pregnant to fly.'

'So the baby would be English?'

'Yes.'

'And you would support it how?'

'The same way that billions of non-billionaires do.'

'Would you have told me?'

'Yes.' She needed the truth from him now and she turned in his arms. 'Are you still here because of the baby?'

'No,' Raúl said. 'I am here because of you.'

She knew he was telling her the truth—not just because he always did, but because of what he said.

'I have had three hellish nights in my life. The first I struggle to speak about, but with you I am starting to. The second was the night after I'd found out about my brother and you were there. I went to bed not thinking about revenge or hate, but about a kiss that went too far and a slap to my cheek. I guess I loved you then, but it felt safer not to admit that.'

'And the third?'

'Finding myself in a nightmare—but not the one I am used to,' Raúl said. 'I was not in a car calling out to my mother. I was not begging her to slow down, and nor was I pleading with her to wake…'

Tears filled her eyes as she imagined it, but she held onto them, knew she would only ever get glimpses of that time and she must piece them together in the quiet of her mind.

'Instead I realised, again, that a woman I loved was gone because of my harsh actions and words. Worse, though. This time it *was* my fault.'

She heard him forgive what his five-year-old self had said as the past was looked at through more mature eyes.

'I went to Angela. She was always the one I went to when I messed up, and I had messed up again. I asked her what to do. I was already on my way to you. It was then that she told me that at least my father had known about the baby… It would seem I was the last to know.'

'I never told her.'

'I'm glad that she guessed. She told my father that morning. I'm glad that he knew, even if I did not.' He looked at her and smiled. 'Opposites attract, Estelle.' He kissed her nose. 'It's law. You can't argue with that.'

'I'm not arguing.'

'Did you hate every dance?' he asked.

She shook her head. 'Of course not.'

'We'll have to get babysitters when we want to go out soon.'

He blew out a breath at the thought of the changes that were to come and she saw that he was smiling.

'Who'd have thought?'

'Not me,' Estelle admitted.

'So, how do you tell your wife you want to marry her all over again?'

'We don't need to get married again,' Estelle said. 'Though a second honeymoon might be nice.'

'Where?'

He was going to make her say it.

'Where?'

'On the yacht.'

Yes, she could get used to that—especially when he made love to her all over again. Especially when he made her laugh about the maid's secret swapping of his DVDs.

No, he had never lied. But he'd never been more honest—and it felt so good.

'Do you think your family will notice a change in us?'

'No.' Estelle smiled. 'They think we met and fell head over heels in love.'

'They were right.' Raúl pulled her to him and then kissed her again. 'We were the only ones who couldn't quite believe it.'

EPILOGUE

IT WAS A beautiful wedding, held on the yacht, which had dropped anchor in Acantilados de Maro-Cerro.

It was Raúl's wedding gift to Gordon for bringing Estelle to him.

The grooms wore white and, contrary to Spanish tradition, there *were* speeches.

'I never thought I'd be standing declaring my love amongst my closest family and friends…' Gordon smiled, and then the dancing started.

Estelle leant against Raúl, feeling the kicks of their baby inside her.

'Is that Gordon's son Ginny is dancing with?' Estelle asked.

'They've been going out for a while.'

'Really?' Estelle smothered a smile. Raúl noticed everything. 'Gordon was once married before—ages ago, apparently.'

'How will they say they met? She can hardly admit she was his father's…' He stopped as Estelle dug him in the ribs. 'Sorry,' Raúl said. 'Sometimes I forget your other life.'

She didn't laugh this time, because the feeling was starting again—like a tight belt pulling around her stomach.

'Do you remember when we stopped here?' Raúl asked.

'When we took out a jet ski and you were scared and trying not to show it.'

'Of course I do.' Estelle attempted to answer normally. 'And I remember when we went snorkeling, and I—'

'Estelle?' He heard her voice break off mid-sentence.

Estelle had been trying to ignore the tightenings, but this one she could not ignore. Raúl's hand moved to her stomach, felt it taut and hard beneath his hands.

'I'll organise a speedboat to take us back to Marbella.'

'It might be ages yet. I don't want to make a fuss.'

'I think it would be a bit more awkward for Gordon if you have the baby here.' He glanced around at the guests and then went to have a word with Alberto, who soon organised transport.

'We are going to head off,' Raúl said when Gordon cornered them. 'Estelle is tired…' But then he couldn't lie— because Estelle was bent over.

'Oh, my!' Gordon was beaming.

'Please,' Estelle begged. 'I don't want everyone to know.'

There was no chance of keeping it quiet as she was helped down to the swimming platform, from where she was guided onto a speedboat. They sped off to the cheers and whistles of the wedding party.

'I wanted to have it in England…'

'I know.' They were supposed to have been flying there the next morning. 'But you wanted to be at the wedding too,' he reminded her.

'I know.'

'You can't have everything,' he teased. 'That's only me.'

She groaned with another pain and buried her face in his neck, wondering how much worse the pains would get, grateful that Raúl was so calm.

He *was* calm—he had everything he wanted right here on this small boat.

He looked up at the cliffs. He had long ago let go of that night, but there was a brief moment of memory just then. It didn't panic him. For a minute he thought of his mother and prayed for her peace.

It was the longest night, and her labour went on well into the next day.

Estelle pushed and dug her nails into his arms, and just when she was sure she could not go on any longer, finally the end was in sight.

'No empujen!'

'Don't push,' Raúl translated.

He had been incredibly composed throughout, but he was starting to worry now, watching the black hair of his infant and realising that soon he would be a father for real.

And then he saw her.

Red, angry, with black hair and fat cheeks.

And as he held her he was more than willing to be completely responsible for this little heart.

The midwife asked if they had a name as she went to write on the wristband and he looked at Estelle. They had chosen a few names, but had opted to wait till the baby was here before they decided. There was one name that had not been suggested till now.

'Gabriella?' Estelle said, and he nodded, unable to speak for a moment. The name that had once meant so much pain was wrapped now in love, and his mother's name would go on.

'Gabriella Sanchez Connolly,' Raúl said.

'She needs a middle name,' Estelle said.

'What about your mother's?' Raúl said, but Estelle already had her mother's name, and thanks to Spanish tradition Connolly was there, too.

Together they held and gazed at their very new daughter, quietly deciding what her full name would be.

'I want to ring Andrew and tell him he's an uncle,' Estelle said, her eyes filling with selfish tears—because though she could not be happier still she wanted to share the news. She wanted her brother to see Gabriella, as she had held Cecelia the day she was born.

'Why would you ring?' Raúl asked. 'They are waiting outside. I will go and bring them in now.'

Raúl stepped out into the waiting room.

His eyes were bloodshot, his hair unkempt, he was unshaven and there was lipstick on his collar—only this time Angela was smiling.

'It's a girl,' Raúl said. 'Both are doing really well,' he said.

Amanda burst into tears and Andrew shook his hand.

'Baby!' Cecelia said, pointing to her little cousin as Estelle showed off the newest arrival to the Connolly clan and thought that Raúl had somehow made an already perfect day even better.

'Come and see,' Raúl said to Angela, who was standing back at the door.

'She's beautiful.' Angela looked down and smiled at the chubby cheeks, seeing the eyes of Luka and Raúl. 'Just perfect—does she have a name?'

'Gabriella,' Raúl said, and looked at the woman who had been like a mother to him, even if it had been from a distance. 'Gabriella Angela Sanchez Connolly.'

Yes, Spanish names could be complicated at times, but they were very simple too.

It was a perfect day, and later came a blissful night, with

Estelle sharing a drink of champagne with her family till Cecelia was drooping in Andrew's arms.

'We're going to get back to the hotel,' Andrew said, looking down at Gabriella. He gave Estelle's hand a squeeze. 'Mum and Dad would have been really proud.'

'I know.'

And then it was just the two of them, lying in bed together, on their first night with Gabriella here.

'There is a text from Luka.' Raúl gave a brief eye-roll as he read the message. 'I have a feeling Angela may have hijacked his phone and typed it.' Raúl's voice was wry. Things were still terribly strained with Luka, but Raúl, very new to being a brother, was trying to work through it.

Not that Luka wanted to.

'You'll get there,' said Estelle.

'Perhaps,' Raúl said.

'Thank you for today.'

Gabriella, who was snuggled up in her cot beside them, made a small noise, and Raúl thought his heart might burst with pride and love as he gazed at his sleeping daughter.

'Thank *you*,' he said. 'I never thought I could feel so much happiness.'

'I meant for bringing my family over. It means so much to me to have them here.'

'I know it does.' He turned his gaze from his daughter to his wife. 'I know, thanks to you, the importance of family—even a difficult one.' He kissed her tired mouth. 'And no matter what happens I am never going to forget it.'

* * * * *

A sneaky peek at next month...

MODERN™

INTERNATIONAL AFFAIRS, SEDUCTION & PASSION GUARANTEED

My wish list for next month's titles...

In stores from 18th October 2013:

❏ Million Dollar Christmas Proposal – Lucy Monroe

❏ The Consequences of That Night – Jennie Lucas

❏ Visconti's Forgotten Heir – Elizabeth Power

❏ A Touch of Temptation – Tara Pammi

In stores from 1st November 2013:

❏ A Dangerous Solace – Lucy Ellis

❏ Secrets of a Powerful Man – Chantelle Shaw

❏ Never Gamble with a Caffarelli – Melanie Milburne

❏ The Rogue's Fortune – Cat Schield

Available at WHSmith, Tesco, Asda, Eason, Amazon and Apple

Just can't wait?

Special Offers

Every month we put together collections and longer reads written by your favourite authors.

Here are some of next month's highlights— and don't miss our fabulous discount online!

On sale 1st November

On sale 1st November

On sale 18th October

Save 20%
on all Special Releases

Find out more at
www.millsandboon.co.uk/specialreleases

*Visit us
Online*

1113/ST/MB440

Come home this Christmas to Fiona Harper

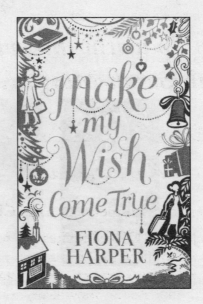

From the author of *Kiss Me Under the Mistletoe* comes a Christmas tale of family and fun. Two sisters are ready to swap their Christmases—the busy super-mum, Juliet, getting the chance to escape it all on an exotic Christmas getaway, whilst her glamorous work-obsessed sister, Gemma, is plunged headfirst into the family Christmas she always thought she'd hate.

www.millsandboon.co.uk

Wrap up warm this winter with Sarah Morgan…

Sleigh Bells in the Snow

Kayla Green loves business and hates Christmas.

So when Jackson O'Neil invites her to Snow Crystal Resort to discuss their business proposal… the last thing she's expecting is to stay for Christmas dinner. As the snowflakes continue to fall, will the woman who doesn't believe in the magic of Christmas finally fall under its spell…?

4th October

www.millsandboon.co.uk/sarahmorgan

MILLS & BOON® Book Club

Join the Mills & Boon Book Club

Want to read more **Modern**™ books?
We're offering you **2 more** absolutely **FREE!**

We'll also treat you to these fabulous extras:

- Exclusive offers and much more!
- FREE home delivery
- FREE books and gifts with our special rewards scheme

Get your free books now!

visit www.millsandboon.co.uk/bookclub
or call Customer Relations on 020 8288 2888

FREE BOOK OFFER TERMS & CONDITIONS
Accepting your free books places you under no obligation to buy anything and you may cancel at any time. If we do not hear from you we will send you 4 stories a month which you may purchase or return to us—the choice is yours. Offer valid in the UK only and is not available to current Mills & Boon subscribers to this series. We reserve the right to refuse an application and applicants must be aged 18 years or over. Only one application per household. Terms and prices are subject to change without notice. As a result of this application you may receive further offers from other carefully selected companies. If you do not wish to share in this opportunity please write to the Data Manager at PO BOX 676, Richmond, TW9 1WU.